"Whatever threat is jeopardizing the peace of this town and the law, you can be sure I'll be out there fighting it." Bree pressed her full lips together.

Jamie wondered what she'd do if he tried to kiss her. His pulse quickened. As unpredictable and unreasonable as she was, she might just shoot him.

Not that kissing those lips wouldn't be worth the risk. Not that he was going to do it. He was in town on serious business. And women were no longer part of his life, anyway. He had too much baggage, too many nightmares. He had no right to bring that into a relationship and mess up somebody else's life along with his.

He was a trained killing machine. That was about it. He planned on living the rest of his life using what skills he had in the service of his country. He stood. "Forget about me and my team."

Although, he was pretty sure he wasn't going to be able to forget about her.

MY SPY

—

DANA MARTON

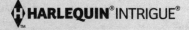

Recycling programs
for this product may
not exist in your area.

ISBN-13: 978-0-373-74774-0

MY SPY

Printed in U.S.A.

ABOUT THE AUTHOR

Dana Marton is the author of more than a dozen fast-paced, action-adventure, romance-suspense novels and a winner of a Daphne du Maurier Award of Excellence. She loves writing books of international intrigue, filled with dangerous plots that try her tough-as-nails heroes and the special women they fall in love with. Her books have been published in seven languages in eleven countries around the world. When not writing or reading, she loves to browse antiques shops and enjoys working in her sizable flower garden, where she searches for "bad" bugs with the skills of a superspy and vanquishes them with the agility of a commando soldier. Every day in her garden is a thriller. To find more information on her books, please visit www.danamarton.com. She loves to hear from her readers and can be reached via email at danamarton@danamarton.com.

Books by Dana Marton

HARLEQUIN INTRIGUE

*Mission: Redemption
**Defending the Crown
***HQ: Texas

CAST OF CHARACTERS

Bree Tridle—When a stalker returns from her past, deputy sheriff Bree Tridle's life is in danger. Dare she accept help from a handsome stranger who has the singular ability to get on her last nerve?

Jamie Cassidy—An undercover operative with a dark past, Jamie is watching the border to catch some terrorists. Seeing Bree in danger doesn't sit well with him, especially since he suspects there might be some serious bad guys after her.

The Coyote—A mysterious and powerful crime lord on the south side of the border. His true identity is unknown.

Katie Tridle—Bree's sister. Since Katie lives with autism, Bree is extra protective of her. No way is she going to let her stalker put Katie in danger.

SDDU—Special Designation Defense Unit. A top-secret commando team established to fight terrorism and other international crime that affects the U.S. The group's existence is known only by a select few. Members are recruited from the best of the best. Jamie Cassidy is part of a six-man team from the SDDU who are stationed on the Texas–Mexican border.

Chapter One

He had two weeks to gain the information he needed to stop terrorists with weapons of mass destruction from entering the country. But everything his six-man team had done so far had been a bust.

Undercover operative Jamie Cassidy sat with his back to the wall in the far corner at the Yellow Armadillo, a seedy, small-town bar on the backstreets of Pebble Creek, Texas. Country music streamed from overhead speakers; the place was dark and dingy, the food was fried within an inch of its life. But the beer was cold, the only nice thing that could be said about the joint.

"So you have no idea who the new boss is?" he asked the scrawny farmhand across the table.

Billy Brunswik fingered the rim of the tattered Stetson on his lap, his eyes on his empty glass. A cowboy tan left the top of his forehead white, the rest of his face several shades darker. His checkered blue shirt was wrinkled and smudged with dirt, as if he'd been wearing it for more than a day or two. He silently shook his head.

Jamie had his own cowboy hat and jeans and shirt to fit in, a far cry from his usual commando gear. In a place like this—a known hangout for smugglers—being spotted as a government man could quickly earn you a bullet in the back.

He waved the perky blonde waitress over for another round for Billy but didn't return her flirty smile. His attention was on the man across the table. "It's tough. Believe me, I know." He waited until the waitress left. "In this economy, and they cut off work. Hell, what are you supposed to do? Who do you go to now?"

"Nobody knows nuthin'." Billy set his empty glass down and wiped his upper lip with the back of his calloused hand, then pulled out a tin of chewing tobacco and tucked a pinch between gum and cheek. "I can barely buy groceries for the girlfriend and me, I'll tell you that."

Jamie watched him for a few seconds, then slid three twenties across the table. "I know how it is."

Billy was on the cash like a duck on a june

bug, the bills disappearing in a flat second. He looked around nervously, licking his crooked yellow front teeth. "I ain't no snitch."

Jamie gave a sympathetic nod. "A man has to live. And I ain't asking for nothing that would get you in trouble. Just need enough to show the boss I've been working." He shrugged, playing the halfhearted customs agent role.

Billy hung his head. "I do work a little," he admitted. "When nobody's lookin'. Just some weed."

"Who do you kick up to?"

"Ain't nobody there since Kenny."

And no matter how hard Jamie pushed the down-on-his-luck farmhand after that, Billy didn't give up anything. Although he did promise to get in touch if things changed.

Developing an asset was a slow and careful business.

Jamie left the man and strode across the bar, looking for familiar faces as he passed the rows of tables. The two border towns his team watched, Hullett and Pebble Creek, had their share of smugglers, most of them lying low these days. He didn't recognize anyone here today.

He paid the waitress at the bar, stepped outside into the scorching heat then shoved his hat on his head and rubbed his eyes. He'd spent the night on border patrol, then most of the morning running down leads. His legs hurt. The doc at Walter Reed called it phantom-limb pain.

He resisted the urge to reach down and rub his prosthetic limbs. It did nothing for the pain, and he hated the feel of the cold steel where his legs should have been.

He strode up to Main Street, came out by the bank and drew a hundred out of the ATM while he was here, since Billy had cleaned him out. Then his gaze caught on the bookstore across the street. Maybe a good read would help him fall asleep. When on duty, his mind focused on work. But when he rested, memories of his dark past pushed their way back into his head. Sleep had a way of eluding him.

He cut across traffic and pushed inside the small indie bookstore, into the welcoming cool of air-conditioning, and strode straight to the mystery section. He picked out a hardboiled detective story, then turned on his heels and came face-to-face with the woman of his dreams.

Okay, the woman of every red-blooded man's dreams.

She was tall and curvy, with long blond hair swinging in a ponytail, startling blue eyes that held laughter and a mouth to kill or die for, depending on what she wished.

His mind went completely blank for a second, while his body sat up and took serious notice.

When his dreams weren't filled with blood and torture and killing, they were filled with sex. He could still do the act—one thing his injury hadn't taken away from him. But he didn't allow himself. He didn't want pity. Foreplay shouldn't start with him taking off his prosthetics—the ultimate mood killer. And he definitely didn't want the questions.

Hell, even he hated touching the damn things. Who wouldn't? He wasn't going to put himself through that humiliation. Wasn't going to put a woman in a position where she'd have to start pretending.

But he dreamed, and his imagination made it good. The woman of his dreams was always the same, an amalgamation of pinup girls that had been burned into his brain during his adolescent years from various magazines he and his brothers had snuck into the house.

And now she was standing in front of him.

The pure, molten-lava lust that shot through his gut nearly knocked him off his feet. And aggravated the hell out of him. He'd spent considerable time suppressing his physical needs so they wouldn't blindside him like this.

"Howdy," she said with a happy, peppy grin

that smoothed out the little crease in her full bottom lip. She had a great mouth, crease or no crease. Made a man think about his lips on hers and going lower.

He narrowed his eyes. Then he pushed by her with a dark look, keeping his face and body language discouraging. Who the hell was she to upset his hard-achieved balance?

He strode up to the counter and paid with cash because he didn't want to waste time punching buttons on the card reader. He didn't want to spend another second in a place where he could be ambushed like this. The awareness of her back somewhere among the rows of books still tingled all across his skin.

"I'm sorry." The elderly man behind the counter handed back the twenty-dollar bill. "I can't take this." He flashed an apologetic smile as he pushed up his horn-rimmed glasses, then tugged down his denim shirt in a nervous gesture. "The scanner kicked it back."

"I just got it from the bank across the street," Jamie argued, not in the mood for delay.

"I'm sorry, sir."

"Everything okay, Fred?" The woman he'd tried to pretend didn't exist came up behind Jamie.

Her voice was as smooth as the kind of top-shelf whiskey the Yellow Armadillo couldn't afford to carry. Its sexy timbre tickled something behind his breastbone. He kept his back to her, against enormous temptation to turn, hoping she'd get the hint to mind her own business.

Then he had to turn, anyway, because next thing he knew she was talking to him.

"I'd be happy to help. How about we go next door and I'll help you figure this out?"

The police station stood next door. All he wanted was to go home and see if he could catch a few winks before his next shift. "I don't think so." He peeled off another twenty, which went through the scanner without trouble. Next thing he knew, Fred was handing back his change.

"I really think we should," the woman insisted.

Apparently, she had trouble with the concept of minding her own business. He shot her a look of disapproval, hoping she'd take the hint.

He tried to look at nothing but her eyes, but all that sparkling blue was doing things to him. Hell, another minute, and if she asked him to eat the damned twenty, he would have probably done it. He caught that thought, pushed back hard.

"Who the hell are you?" He kept his tone at a level of surly that had taken years to perfect.

The cheerleader smile never even wavered

as she pulled her badge from her pocket and flashed it at him. "Brianna Tridle. Deputy sheriff."

Oh, hell.

He looked her over more thoroughly: the sexy snakeskin boots, the hip-hugging jeans, the checkered shirt open at the neck, giving a hint of the top curve of her breasts. His palms itched for a feel. If there was such a thing as physical perfection, she was it.

Any guy who had two brain cells to rub together would have gone absolutely anywhere with her.

Except Jamie Cassidy.

"I'm in a hurry."

"Won't take but a minute." She tilted her head, exposing the creamy skin of her neck just enough to bamboozle him. "I've been having a hard time with counterfeit bills turning up in town lately. I'd really appreciate the help. I'll keep it as quick as possible, I promise." The smile widened enough to reveal some pearly white teeth.

Teeth a man wouldn't have minded running his tongue along before kissing her silly.

Another man.

Certainly not Jamie.

Okay, so she was the deputy sheriff. The sheriff, Kenny Davis, had been killed recently.

He'd been part of the smuggling operation Jamie's team was investigating. A major player, actually.

After that, Ryder McKay, Jamie's team leader, had looked pretty closely at the Pebble Creek police department. The rest of them came up squeaky clean. A shame, really. Jamie definitely felt like his world would be safer with Brianna Tridle locked away somewhere far from him.

She was too chirpy by half.

He didn't like chirpy.

But if she wasn't a suspect, she could be an ally—if he played his cards right. Although poker wasn't the first thing to spring to mind when he thought about playing with her. He could no longer feel the air-conditioning. In fact, it seemed the AC might have broken since he'd come in. The place felt warm suddenly. Hot, even.

He loosened the neck of his shirt. "Fine. Five minutes."

He held the door for her, regretting it as she flashed another gut punch of a smile. She better not read anything into that basic courtesy. He'd been raised right, that was all. He couldn't help it. He wasn't falling for her charms, no way, he thought as she walked in front of him, hips swinging.

The gentle sway held him mesmerized for a minute. Then he blinked hard as he finally focused on one specific spot. Was that a small firearm tucked under her waistband, covered by her shirt? Hard to tell with his eyes trying to slide lower.

He looked more carefully. Damn if the slight bulge wasn't a weapon. She'd been armed the entire time and he'd never noticed. He was seriously losing it.

He drew in a slow breath as they walked into the station. On second thought, forget developing her as an asset. Working with her would probably be more trouble than it was worth.

He was going to tell Brianna Tridle where, when and exactly how he'd come into possession of the stupid twenty-dollar bill in question. Then he was walking out and not looking back. If he had even a smidgen of luck coming to him, he'd never see her again.

"I REALLY APPRECIATE this." Bree measured up the cowboy with the bad attitude.

Not a real Texas cowboy, actually. He was missing the Texas twang, his general accent making it difficult to pin down from where he hailed. And he wore combat boots with his jeans. It threw off his cowboy swagger. He had shadows all around him, his aura a mixture of dangerous and sexy. He was hot enough to give women heart palpitations on his worst day.

Not that that sort of thing affected her. She was a seasoned law enforcement officer. "And your name is?"

"Jamie Cassidy." He didn't offer his hand, or even a hint of a smile as he scanned the station.

She'd bet good money he didn't miss many details. Fine. She was proud of the place, clean and organized. The dozen people working there were the finest in South Texas. She would trust each and every one of them to have her back.

While he examined her station, she examined him.

He stood tall, well built, his dirty-blond hair slightly mussed as he took his hat off. When he ran his fingers through it in an impatient gesture, Bree's own fingertips tingled.

He had the face of a tortured angel, all angles and masculine beauty. His chocolate-brown eyes seemed permanently narrowed and displeased. Especially as he took in the metal detectors she'd had installed just last week.

Lena, the rookie officer manning the scanner, held out a gray plastic tray for him.

Bree offered a smile. "We just upped our security. If you could hand over anything metal in your pockets and walk through, I'd appreciate it."

She was in charge of the station until the new sheriff was elected. They'd had an incident recently with a drunk housewife who'd come in to file a complaint against her husband, then ended up shooting a full clip into the ceiling to make sure they believed her when she said she *would* shoot the bastard if he came into her new double-wide one more time with muddy boots.

She'd been a bundle of booze and wild emotions—the very opposite of Jamie Cassidy, who seemed the epitome of cold and measured.

He scowled as he dropped his cell phone, handful of change and car keys into the small plastic tray. "I'm going to set the alarm off." He tapped his leg. "Prosthesis."

That was it, then, Bree thought as she watched him. The reason why his walk had been off a smidgen. "Not a problem, Lena," she told the rookie, who was staring at him with dreamy eyes. "I'll pat him down."

"No." His face darkened as his gaze cut to hers.

They did a long moment of the staring-each-other-down thing. Then his lips narrowed as he fished around in his shirt pocket and pulled out a CBP badge.

Customs and Border Protection. *And the plot thickens.* She tilted her head as she considered him. Why not show the badge sooner?

Maybe it was a fake. She'd worked pretty closely with CBP for the past couple of years. She'd never seen him before. If she had, she would have definitely remembered him.

She widened her smile. Defusing tension in a bad situation always worked better than escalating it. "I need to check you just the same. New procedure. Sorry."

For a second he looked like he might refuse and simply walk away from her. She kept her hand near her firearm at her back, ready to stop him. She preferred to do things the easy way, but she could do it the hard way if needed. Up to him.

But then he seemed to change his mind and held out his arms to the side. She wondered if he knew that his smoldering look of resentment only made him look sexier.

"It'll only take a second." She ran her fingers along his arms first, lightly. Plenty of muscle. If he did change his mind and began causing trouble, she would definitely need her service weapon.

She moved her hands to his torso and found more impressive muscles there. She could feel the heat of his body through his shirt and went faster when her fingertips began to tingle again, a first for her during pat down. What on earth was wrong with her today? She tried to focus on what she was doing. Okay, no shoulder holster, no sidearm here.

"Almost done." She squatted as she moved down his legs, pausing at the sharp transition where the living flesh gave way to rigid metal. *Both* of his legs were missing. Her gaze flew up to his.

He looked back down at her with something close to hate—a proud man who didn't like his weaknesses seen.

"Enough." He stepped back.

But she stepped after him. "One more second."

Awareness tingled down her spine as she pulled up and reached around his waist, almost as if she were hugging him. And there, tucked behind his belt, she found a small, concealed weapon.

She removed the firearm carefully, pointing it down, making sure her fingers didn't come near the trigger. "When were you going to tell me about this?" She checked the safety. *On.* Okay.

"I'm so used to carrying, I forgot," he lied to her face.

Which ticked her off a little.

She dropped the weapon into the gray plastic tray Lena was holding. "You can claim these on your way out." If she let him leave. "This way."

They went through the detector, which did go off, as he'd promised. Curiosity, wariness and even some unwanted attraction warred inside her as she led him into interview room A at the end of the hallway. He was not your average Joe. This man had a story. She wanted to know what it was.

"How about I get us something cold to drink?"

He didn't look impressed with her hospitality as he scanned the small white room. "I'm in a hurry."

She left him anyway, and swung by Lena on her way to the vending machine. "Let me see that." She took his weapon, grabbed two sodas then stopped by her office and ran the gun.

Unregistered firearm. On a hunch, she called her friend Gina at the local CBP office. "Hey, you got someone over there by the name of Jamie Cassidy?"

"Not that I know off the top of my head. Why? Anything to do with the counterfeiting thing you're working?"

"Don't know yet. Might be nothing. I'll talk to you later." She hung up and walked by Lena again, looking at Jamie Cassidy's car keys in the plastic tray.

"You'll need a warrant to look in his car,"

Lena remarked, now sitting by her computer, answering citizen queries.

"Or his permission. Least I can do is try," Bree said as she walked away.

Mike was coming from the evidence room. "What you up to?"

"Picked up someone with a fake twenty."

"Need help?" He was a few weeks from retirement, but not the type to sit back and count off the days. He was always first to offer help and never said a word if he had to work late.

"Thanks. But I think I can handle him." She hoped. She was ready to roll up the counterfeiting thing.

She was sick of the recent crime wave in her town lately: a rash of burglaries, several acts of unusual vandalism and sabotage, arson even, and then the counterfeit bills showing up suddenly. Whatever she had to do, she was going to put an end to it.

She grabbed her shoulder holster from the back of her chair, shrugged into the leather harness and stuck her weapon into the holster to keep it within easier reach. Time to figure out who Jamie Cassidy was and if he'd come to town to cause trouble.

She had a sudden premonition that prying that out of him wasn't going to be easy. She'd been a cop long enough to know when somebody was lying, and the man waiting for her in interview room A definitely had his share of secrets.

HE WAS SITTING in an interrogation room, fully aroused. That was a first, Jamie thought wryly. Because, of course, she'd *had* to put her hands on him. At least she hadn't noticed his condition; she'd been too focused on his weapon.

He leaned back in the uncomfortable metal chair. The place was small, the cement brick walls freshly painted white, the old tile floor scuffed.

The metal door stood open, but the station was full of uniforms. He wouldn't get far if he tried to walk out, not without violence, and he wanted to avoid that if possible. He watched as the deputy sheriff reappeared at the end of the hallway, her gaze immediately seeking out his.

And there it came again, that punch of heat in the gut.

"Stupid," he said under his breath, to snap himself out of it.

He'd never been like this. Back when he'd been whole, he'd enjoyed the fairer sex as much as the next guy. Since he'd been crippled, he kept to himself. He was half machine, half human. Who the hell would want to touch that?

Yet she'd touched him and hadn't flinched

away. She'd felt his prosthetics and her face had registered surprise, but not pity. He pushed that thought aside. What would Miss Perfection know about physical deformity?

He watched as a uniformed cop, dragging a loud-mouthed drunk, headed her off halfway down the hall.

"No needles," the drunk protested, then swore a blue streak, struggling against the man who held him, trying for a good swing, the movement nearly knocking him off his unsteady feet.

Brianna Tridle smiled sweetly.

Yeah, that was going to work. The man needed someone to put the fear of God into him. Jamie could have gotten the job done in three seconds flat. Possibly two. He relaxed and got ready to enjoy watching the deputy sheriff fail.

"Come on now, Pete." She kept up the all-is-well-with-the-world, we're-all-friends routine. "Big, tough guy like you. Remember when you had that wire snap at work and cut your leg open? You didn't make a sound all the way to the hospital when I took you in. Pretty impressive."

The drunk pulled himself together a little and gave her a sheepish look. "It's just the needles. You know I can't stand them, darlin'."

"Tell you what. You do the blood test, I'll drive you home. You won't have to wait here until Linda gets off shift."

"Can't give no blood." He shook his head stubbornly. "I'm dizzy. Haven't even eaten all day."

"I bet Officer Roberts hasn't had lunch yet, either. How about you swing by the drive-through and grab a couple of hamburgers? On me."

The drunk went all googly-eyed. "You'll always be a queen to me, darlin'," he promised, and this time followed Officer Roberts obediently as he was led away.

Jamie stared. *Enforcing the law with sweet talk.*

What kind of monkey-circus police station was this? And then he stilled as he realized he was even now sitting in an interrogation room, where he'd had no intention of being. Hell, the woman had done it to him!

He glared at her with all the resentment he felt as she came in with a couple of drinks. He was out of here.

"Got the money out of the ATM at the bank across the street five minutes ago. You can check their security video." He rose. "That's all I know."

She put a can of soda in front of him with

that smile that seemed to have the ability to addle everyone's brain around her. She sat, folding her long legs under her seat. "Just a few minutes. Please?" she asked very nicely. "As a favor from one law enforcement drone to another."

Establishing common ground in thirty seconds flat. Nice work, he had to admit. He sat, but only because he was beginning to be intrigued.

"What do you do, exactly, at CBP?" She fitted her supremely kissable lips to the can as she drank, keeping an eye on him.

"I'm on a special team," he said, more than a little distracted.

"Dealing with?"

"Special stuff."

She laughed, the sound rippling right through him. He resented that thoroughly.

"Why do you carry an unregistered firearm instead of your service weapon?" she asked as pleasantly as if she was inquiring about his health.

She got that already, did she? A part of him was impressed, a little. Maybe she wasn't just surface beauty.

"Took it off someone this morning. Haven't had a chance yet to turn it in," he lied through his teeth. He was in town as part of an undercover commando team. What they did and how they did it was none of her business.

She smiled as if she believed his every word. "All right, that's it, then," she said brightly. "I better clear you out of here so you can get back to work. I know you guys are busy beyond belief."

She stood, taking her drink with her. "Just to make sure I have all my *T*s crossed and *I*s dotted, would you mind if I took a quick glance at your car?" she added, as if it was an afterthought. "With all this counterfeit stuff I'm struggling with..." She gave a little shrug that another man would have found endearing. "It's really helpful to be able to cross people completely off the list."

"Go ahead," he said, regretting it the next second. But part of him wanted to test her. No way in hell she was going to find the secret compartment that he himself built. "It's a black SUV in front of the bank." He gave her his plate number. "You already have the keys."

She walked out, ensuring him of her gratitude and sincere appreciation. And this time, she closed the door behind her. Which locked automatically.

And just like that, he was in custody.

His mouth nearly gaped at her effortless efficiency.

He had to admit, if he was normal, if he was the type who believed in love, she would be the exact woman he might be tempted to fall in love with.

Of course, with everything she had going for her, chances were she was already married. No wedding ring—he couldn't believe he'd looked—but people in law enforcement often skipped that. No reason to advertise to the bad guys that you had a weakness, a point where you could be hurt.

Married. *There.* He found the thought comforting. He liked the idea of her completely out of his reach. Otherwise, the thought of her would drive him crazy during those long nights when he couldn't sleep.

He waited.

Looked around the small room.

Looked at the locked door.

It'd been a while since he'd been locked up and tortured, but the more he sat in the interrogation room, the more uneasy he felt. *It's not like that.* He swallowed back the memories. Rubbed his knees.

But a cold darkness seemed to fill the room around him little by little, pushing him to his feet. *Think about something else. Think about work.*

Plenty there to figure out. His six-man team was putting the brakes on a serious smuggling operation that planned on bringing terrorists, along with their weapons of mass destruction, into the country, information that had been gained on an unrelated South American op.

To stop the terrorists, his team had to work their way up the chain of command in a multinational criminal organization. They'd gotten the three low-level bosses who ran the smugglers on the United States side of the border. What they needed now was the identity of the Coyote, the big boss who ran things on the other side.

He paced the room, forcing himself to focus on what they knew so far. But too soon his thoughts returned to Brianna Tridle. He moved to the door to look out the small window through the wire-reinforced glass. What he saw didn't make him happy.

She was coming back in with a uniformed cop, carrying his arsenal, down to his nightvision goggles that had been hidden in a separate secret compartment from the rest. She called out to the handful of people in the office as she deposited the weaponry on a desk.

He couldn't hear her, but he could read her

sexy lips. He was pretty sure she'd just said *terror suspect*.

Oh, hell. That definitely didn't bode well for him.

Chapter Two

"Officer Delancy here is going to take your fingerprints," Bree informed Jamie Cassidy, if that was his real name, once she was back in the interview room with him, feeling a lot more cautious suddenly than the first time around.

"I noticed earlier that you had a wallet in your pocket. I'd appreciate it if you handed that over, please." She kept as pleasant an expression on her face as possible, even if she felt far from smiling.

The kind of weapons he had in his SUV were definitely not standard government issue that CBP would use. And they were far too heavy duty for the kind of criminals she usually saw around these parts. He didn't just have weapons—he had an arsenal with him. For what purpose?

"I need to make a phone call," he demanded, instead of complying.

"Maybe later." If he *was* a domestic terrorist,

he could set off a bomb with a phone call. She wasn't going to take chances until she knew more about him. "Let's do those prints first and have a little talk. Then we'll see about the phone."

He scowled at her, looking unhappier by the second. An accomplishment, since he'd been in a pretty sour mood even when she'd first laid eyes on him.

"How about we talk about your weapons first?"

He held her gaze. "How did you find them?"

He clearly hadn't thought she would. At the beginning of her career, it had annoyed her that men tended to underestimate her. Then she'd realized that it was an advantage.

"Just came back from special training with the CBP. They spent three entire days on tips and tricks for spotting secret compartments. Same training you received, I assume? Since you claim you work for them?"

Smuggling had been getting out of hand in the area until a sudden recent drop she didn't think would last. And now with the counterfeit money nonsense… She needed skills that would help her put an end to that. As she watched him, she wondered if he was a CBP agent gone bad. It happened.

"You're making a mistake here."

"Oh, Lord," she said easily. "I make at least ten a day, for sure." She smiled. "Why are you in Pebble Creek, Jamie?"

"I told you. I consult for CBP," he said morosely, but sat back down and let Delancy take his fingerprints.

Consulting now, was it? His story was subtly changing. There was more here, something he wasn't telling her.

"And you needed those guns for..."

"I spend a lot of time on the border."

"Doing what?"

"Monitoring smuggling."

Or helping it along, most likely.

Sheriff Davis was dead, the new sheriff elections mere weeks away. She'd been away for training and out of the loop, way too much dropping on her lap the day she'd come back. Like counterfeit twenties showing up.

She'd notified the CIA as soon as she'd caught the first. They were sending an agent before the end of the week to investigate. Acid bubbled in her stomach every time she thought of that. She wasn't a big fan of outsiders messing around in her town.

And if that wasn't enough, now she had Jamie Cassidy to deal with. She was starting to feel the beginnings of a headache.

He was watching her, his eyes hard, his face

closed, his masculine mouth pressed into a line—not exactly a picture of cooperation. If this went the way she thought it would, she'd be here all day and then some. Which meant she'd have to call her sister and let her know she'd be late. Not a good thing with Katie being so bad with even the slightest change in her routine.

"How long have you been in town?" she asked as Delancy left with the fingerprint kit, closing the door behind her.

"A couple of weeks."

Which coincided with the counterfeit money showing up.

He rubbed the heels of his hands over his knees, drawing her attention there. How much did she know about what was really under his jeans, anyway? She'd felt metal. But was all of that his prosthetics?

She stood to walk around the desk. "Would you mind rolling up your pants?" she asked in her friendliest tone. "In light of the weapons we found in your car, I'd feel more comfortable if I made a full search. Just to set my mind at ease."

If he'd been cold before, he went subzero now, his gaze turning to black ice. Every muscle in his body tensed. She'd definitely hit a nerve.

Would he hit back? She was ready to defend herself, not that she was looking forward to tackling him. He looked strong, quick and capable.

She should have asked Delancy to stay as backup, she thought too late. Jamie was already on his feet.

ANGER AND HUMILIATION washed over Jamie as he stood. He'd played along long enough. He didn't have time for this. "You need to let me make that call."

The next thing he knew, he was shoved face-first into the wall, his right hand twisted up behind his back, his cheek rubbing into the brick. Air whooshed out of his lungs, more from surprise than anything else.

Her transformation from sweet to tough cop was pretty spectacular and stunned him more than a little. For a second her body pressed against his full-length from the back, her soft breasts flattened against his ribs. Another place, another time... Heat and awareness shot through him, pure lust drowning out the aggravation that she would try to manhandle him.

He could have put her down. He could have put her down hard.

But she was an officer of the law, and they were on the same side. And frankly, he was beginning to respect her skills.

"Take it easy," he said. "I'm cooperating."

He let her pull down his other hand and put plastic restraints on him, even if the thought of being tied up made him uneasy. Any undercover commando who couldn't get out of plastic restraints in under a minute needed to quit. He said nothing when she edged his boots apart with her foot.

Then she bent and grabbed on to the hem of his jeans, and that set his teeth on edge. "That's not necessary. I'm not the enemy."

She rolled the denim up briskly. "Just a quick check. Then you give me that number you want to call and I'll call for you. How about that?"

Over his dead body. She called Ryder and Jamie would never live it down that he'd gotten nabbed and interrogated by Deputy Sheriff Hot Chick.

He held still as she moved his pant leg up. He knew what she would see: cold steel alloy, nothing human, a well-engineered machine. He'd received his prosthetics as a major favor from a friend of the colonel his team reported to. It was the best technology Olympic athletes used, taken up another notch. A prototype, the first and only set to receive the designation combat ready.

"Fancy hardware," she commented as she covered up his left leg and moved on to the right. "How did this happen?"

None of her business. "Car accident." He said the first thing that came to mind.

"I would have thought war injury." She finished and straightened, expertly sliding her hand into his pocket and retrieving his wallet. "You move like a soldier."

And suddenly he had enough of her prying into his business. He twisted his wrist to expose the link on his metal watchband that he kept sharp. Another twist, applying pressure to the right places, and he was free.

He reached for her as he turned, caught her by surprise and had her trapped against the wall in a split second, holding her hands at either side of her head, preventing her from going for her weapon.

Their faces were inches from each other, their bodies nearly touching. She stared at him with wide-eyed surprise that quickly turned to anger, then back to calm strength again, the transition fascinating to observe.

God, she was even more beautiful up close— those sparkling blue eyes and all that flawless skin.

"Not a smart move," she said calmly, the words drawing his gaze to the crease in her bottom lip that begged to be kissed. "I call out and there'll be half a dozen officers in here in a second."

"Why don't you?" He knew the answer, the exact same reason why he hadn't given her the number to call Ryder at the office. She didn't want to embarrass herself.

Her cell phone rang in her pocket.

He thought about kissing her, which was really stupid. He held her for another long second before he stepped back and let her go as a gesture of good faith, but took his wallet back.

She pulled her phone out with one hand, her gun with the other, pointing it at the middle of his chest.

She glared at him as she took the call. "Yes. Yes, sir," she said, the look on her face stunned at first, then quickly turning speculative. She lowered her gun. Her sparkling blue eyes narrowed when the call ended, and she turned her full attention back to him.

She stepped around to put the desk between them once again. "Want to guess who that was?"

He raised an eyebrow.

"Homeland Security. I've been ordered to release you immediately, without any further questions. Want to tell me what that's about?"

He winced. He would rather have that nobody know about his brief time in Brianna Tridle's custody, but, hell, he'd take whatever break he could get at this stage.

He sauntered by her on his way to the door. "Looks like you won't get to keep me. Life is full of disappointments, Deputy Sheriff."

HE ALMOST DIDN'T even mind having to see her again, Jamie thought as he ran a quick background search on her once he was back at his office that night, after having caught a brief nap at his apartment.

She hadn't returned his weapons, probably just to spite him. The orders on the phone had been only about releasing him, she'd said. He could claim his property after a twenty-four-hour waiting period, some rule she'd made up on the fly, he was sure.

"So she hauled you in?" Shep, one of his teammates, was asking with a little too much glee.

They worked out of a bulletproof office trailer in the middle of nowhere, close enough to the border to be able to reach it within minutes, far enough from prying eyes in town.

They had a pretty simple setup: one office for Ryder McKay, the team leader, an interrogation room, a bathroom and a small break room in the back, the rest of the space taken up by desks for the six-man team.

Ryder was locked up in his office, on the phone. The rest of the team was out.

Jamie shrugged as he scrolled down the screen.

"She questioned you?"

"Interrogation room." He spit out the two words as if they were broken glass in his mouth. He read the search results on his screen, scanning the scores of photos of her. *Miss Brianna Tridle accepts her crown.* She'd been Miss Texas. No joke.

She'd been younger—different hair, more makeup, but the smile was the same. He felt a tug in places that hadn't tugged in a long time, just looking at her on the screen.

"Handcuffs?" Shep asked.

He refused to answer, opening the next document that detailed everything from her family circumstances to her education. She was single, the sole guardian of one Katie Tridle, twenty-three years old.

Sister?

There was something there, he thought. Normally a person didn't need a guardian at twenty-three.

"Seriously, she had you in handcuffs?" Shep gave a belly laugh. "Oh, man, I would have given money to see that. Why didn't you just call in?"

Because she wouldn't let me, was the answer, words he wasn't about to say. He shut down his computer instead and pushed to his feet. "Patrol time, funny boy. Move it."

Shep picked up his handgun and shoved it into his holster, grinning all the way. It burned Jamie's temper that he had to get his backup weapon out of his drawer because most of his stuff was in the deputy sheriff's custody.

"Good thing she ran your prints and the flags went off in the system." Shep was having way too much fun with the incident to let it go, giving another gloating smirk as he got into his own SUV while Jamie hopped into his.

Yeah, flags had gone off. Homeland Security had called. They'd called both Brianna Tridle and Ryder at the office, unfortunately.

Jamie turned on radio contact as they pulled out of the parking lot. "How are you doing following up on the Kenny Davis angle?" he asked, ready to change the topic of conversation.

"Running into a lot of dead ends."

The Pebble Creek sheriff had been killed in a confrontation with Mo, another teammate, when the sheriff had gotten involved in the smuggling and kidnapped a little boy to use as leverage to regain a drug shipment he'd lost.

Mo did gain some clues out of his investigation: a code name, Coyote, the head of the smuggling operations on the other side of the border, and a date, October 13.

Something, but not enough. They needed to unravel the Coyote's identity and take him into custody, and they needed to figure out what the date meant.

"You think October 13 is the transfer?" He asked the same question they'd asked each other a dozen times since Mo had come up with the date.

"What else?"

"Why would the sheriff reveal it?"

"A sudden pang of patriotism? He knew at the end that he was dying. Money had been his main motivator for going bad. At that last moment, he knew money was no longer any good to him. He did this one thing to appease his conscience."

That made sense. But October 13 was only three weeks away. They had credible intelligence that several terrorists, along with some weapons of mass destruction, were going to cross this section of the border, the few hundred miles they were patrolling and investigating.

Now they had the date. Hopefully.

They needed an exact location.

To get that, they needed to find the Coyote.

"We'll catch as many smugglers as we can. One of them will lead us to the boss on the other side. He'll have the details of the transfer. Once we have him, I'm not worried. We'll get what we need out of him." Shep was more optimistic than Jamie.

"The smugglers we catch are small potatoes. None of them had a straight line to the Coyote so far."

"Patience is the name of the game."

Not one of his strengths, Jamie silently admitted.

They could have called in the National Guard and closed down the border in this area. But the bad guys would see that and simply bring over the terrorists and their weapons someplace else.

Which was why Jamie's six-man team was handling things quietly. According to their cover, they were here to observe illegal border activity and make budget recommendations to policy makers, while closely working with the CBP. In reality, they were a small, fast-hitting unit of a larger undercover commando team that protected national security all over the globe.

They wanted the terrorists to have no idea that they were expected. They wanted the bastards to come as planned so they could be apprehended and neutralized, taken out of the action for good—the only real solution.

Jamie and Shep talked about that and strategy as they reached the border, then radioed Keith and Mo to return to the office. The night shift was in place.

The full moon had come up, illuminating the landscape: some limited grazing land with large patches of arid ground thrown in that grew nothing but prickly pear and mesquite.

The Rio Grande flowed to the south of them, its dark waters glinting in the moonlight. Cicadas sang in the bushes. Up way ahead, deer were coming in to drink, but hearing the two cars, they darted away.

The place could look so peaceful and serene, belying how much trouble this little strip of land was causing on a regular basis lately.

Jamie pulled into a mesquite grove to observe for a while. Shep drove ahead and disappeared from sight after a few minutes. They were at one of the known crossing spots where the river was wide and the water low, the crossing relatively easy.

He got out his binoculars and used those for the first scan, then switched to his old, cracked night-vision goggles he'd grabbed from the office. He was mostly panning the river's southern bank, so he almost missed the three men who stole forward from the bushes on his other side, carrying oversize backpacks and an inflatable raft.

"Got three here," he said into the radio to warn Shep.

"Be right back."

Jamie didn't wait for him. He started his car and gunned the engine, caught the trio halfway between the bushes and the water, squealed to a stop then jumped out, aiming his weapon as he rushed forward while they scattered.

"Guns on the ground! Hands in the air! Now!"

But the idiots seemed to find courage in the fact that they outnumbered him three to one. The nearest one took a shot at him.

Jamie ducked, ran forward and fired back, aiming for the extremities. They needed information, which dead men couldn't give.

He hit the guy in the leg and the smuggler went down, then Jamie was on top of him, maybe a little rougher than he had to be. His already damaged night-vision goggles broke and fell into the dirt.

Disarming the idiot took a minute, cuffing him another as the man struggled pretty hard while swearing and complaining about his injury.

"I'll feel sorry for you later." Jamie finished securing him. "Now shut up."

By the time he was done, the one who had the raft was at the edge of the water, the other one running in the opposite direction, back into the bushes where they probably had a vehicle hidden.

"Halt!" he called after him, not that the guy obeyed.

Jamie swore as he pushed to his feet. He'd already taken one down. He could have waited for Shep to go after the others together. But he wasn't in the habit of holding anything back.

He took after the guy who was going for the getaway car. With his prosthetics, he was no good in water, a weakness he hated.

He caught sight of Shep's car flying back, kicking up dust, just as the man he was chasing turned for a second and squeezed off another shot at Jamie.

He slowed, steadied his arm and shot back, aiming at the guy's gun and hitting it, a miracle considering the distance and lack of light. Then he darted forward once again, after the man who had already disappeared in the bushes.

The brush he entered was as tall as he was in places so he slowed, watching for movement up ahead. Nothing. The moon sliding behind a stray cloud didn't help. He had his high-powered flashlight clipped to his belt. Too bad turning that on would just make him a target.

Waiting for Shep and hunting as a team would have been smarter, but once again something—

a need to prove himself, pride—pushed him forward.

He moved slowly, step by step, careful not to trip.

Somewhere behind him, Shep beeped his horn to let him know he got his man. That blare turned out to be Jamie's undoing.

He didn't hear the smuggler jump out of the bushes on his right, so he caught the collapsible paddle full in the face.

Pain shot up his nose and into his brain. He sprinted after the bastard anyway, shaking his head to clear it. The uneven ground tried to trip him; he focused on his balance, on closing the distance.

The man dropped his backpack and picked up speed.

Jamie didn't slow to see what he'd been carrying. That could wait.

Dark shadows surrounded them; there was no other sound but their boots slapping on the ground and their harsh breathing. Thorny bushes tore at him, ripping flesh and fabric. He paid no mind to anything but the man in front of him.

When he came close enough, he dove forward. They went down hard onto gravelly ground, rolled. Jamie was stronger, but the guy could maneuver his legs easier. A few minutes passed before he could subdue the smuggler.

"What's your name?" He flipped the guy onto his stomach and yanked the plastic cuff around his wrists. "What are you doing here? Who do you work for?"

But the man didn't respond, just snarled with impotent fury.

Jamie pushed himself up with his hands, then stood, the movement ungainly. Walking and running were his strengths; other things still didn't go as smoothly as he would have liked. He pulled the guy to standing and drew his gun at last to speed things up. "Talk and walk."

The guy did neither, so Jamie shoved him forward.

He picked up the backpack on their way back to the SUV. Judging from the metallic clanking, it held weapons, probably a few dozen small handguns.

Drugs and illegal immigrants were smuggled north; guns and money were smuggled south, in ever increasing quantities, fueling massive empires of crime on both sides and causing untold human misery.

The three they'd caught tonight were a drop in the bucket.

"Got him. Coming out." He called a warning before stepping out of the cover of the bushes.

Shep had been waiting. He lowered his weapon. Looked like he'd already stashed the other two guys in the back of his SUV. He holstered his gun as Jamie came closer.

"You okay? Your nose doesn't look too good."

"Feels like it's been driven into my brain." It really did. He was seeing a couple of extra stars than what were in the sky tonight.

"Broken?"

"Nah." But his cheekbone might have gotten cracked. He flexed his jaw. His face burned like hell.

"Could have waited for me."

Yeah, they were a team. *Whatever*. Just because he was no longer whole didn't mean he couldn't handle a chase by himself. Although that probably wasn't what Shep had meant.

He drew a deep breath. After his injury, he'd spent some time in the darkest pit of depression. Then he'd gotten his new legs and…fine, he'd been overcompensating. "We got them. That's what counts, right?"

Shep was panning the brush with his spotlight. "Did you find their car?"

"Didn't get that far. Has to be back there somewhere. I don't think they walked far." The man he'd chased down had had plenty of energy left in him for a good sprint.

"I'll go and take a look." Shep took off running, keeping both his flashlight and his weapon out.

Jamie shoved the smuggler he'd caught up against his SUV, searched the man's pockets for ID but found nothing but a small bag of weed. He locked the guy in the back of the car then went through the backpack and came up with three dozen brand-new small arms: Ruger .380, the perfect size to be carried concealed.

A small-time operation, but something. These three had to have a link on the other side. And that link would have an uplink. Follow the trail, and it might lead to the elusive Coyote.

He stayed on patrol while Shep ran the smugglers in, bringing Mo back with him so Mo could take the smugglers' car for a thorough search and fingerprinting. They would follow even the smallest lead. The stakes were too high. There were no unimportant details.

They kept an eye out for others. Sometimes smugglers worked in separate teams. They figured if one team got caught, the others would slip through while the border patrol was busy with the unlucky ones.

But the rest of the night went pretty quietly, the borderlands deserted. When Keith and Ray came to take over at dawn, Jamie drove back to his apartment to catch some sleep. His ringing phone woke him around midmorning.

"A friend of yours stopped by to see me earlier," Ryder, the team leader, said on the other end, sounding less than happy.

Jamie tried to unscramble his brain as he sat up and reached for his prosthetics. "Who?"

"Brianna Tridle."

An image of her long legs and full lips slammed into his mind. Okay, now he was wide awake.

"She kept calling up the chain at CBP until they gave her our contact number. Tracked us down from there. She's demanding to be involved in our investigation. If her town and her people are part of whatever our mission is here, as she put it, she wants in."

"How did she take being disappointed?" With her looks, she probably didn't often experience a man saying no to her. Jamie almost wished he could have been there to see when Ryder had done it.

But Ryder said, "Actually, I agreed."

"Say that again?" His hand halted over the straps.

"She grew up around here, knows everyone. People respect her. Record clean as a whistle. We're pressed for time. She could be an asset."

"More like a pain in the asset."

"Possibly. She's pretty protective of her town. In any case, I don't plan on that being my problem," he added cheerfully.

A dark premonition settled over Jamie, immediately justified as Ryder said, "Since you're the one who got her all riled up, you'll be her liaison on the team."

"I don't think it's a good idea to involve her."

"You have my permission to try to talk her out of it. Tomorrow. Right now I need you to drive up to San Antonio. I got a new name from one of the men you and Shep caught last night on the border. Rico Marquez. He's a known gangbanger."

Which translated to: be ready for anything.

He was just as likely to come back with Rico as he was with a bullet in his back.

"Want someone to go with you? I could pull Keith from border detail," Ryder offered. "This is a pretty promising lead."

"Nah," he said, unable, once again, to shake the need to prove himself, even if nobody but him thought that was necessary. "I can handle it."

Chapter Three

Jamie tracked Rico to an abandoned warehouse where the man was apparently hiding out at the moment due to the fact that a rival gang member was hunting him. Information unwittingly supplied by his mother, who'd thought Jamie had come to help her son.

Jamie picked the lock on the rusted emergency door on the side of the building and eased inside little by little, as silently as he could manage. The temperature had to be close to a hundred; there was definitely no air-conditioning here. The cavernous place smelled like dust and machine grease.

The carcass of a giant and complicated-looking piece of machinery took up most of the floor; the ceiling was thirty feet high, at least. A metal walkway ringed the building high up on the wall, and some sort of an office was tucked under the corrugated metal roof in the back.

Jamie caught sight of a faint, flickering light

up there—a TV?—so he moved that way. Where the hell were the stairs?

He walked forward slowly, carefully, listening for any noise that might warn him that he wasn't alone down here. Nothing.

Once he was closer to the back wall, he could hear the muted sounds of the TV upstairs. Good. Maybe they wouldn't hear him coming.

Now all he needed was to find a way up. He wished he had more light down at ground level, but all the windows were up high, just under the roof, and all were covered with enough grime to let through precious little light.

There were a million hiding places for someone to wait to ambush him. Then again, he'd also have plenty of cover if it came to a close-quarters shootout in here.

He scanned all the dark corners and found the stairs at last, hiding behind a bundle of foot-wide pipes that ran up along the wall. He approached it with as much care as possible.

The corner was a perfect place to ambush someone if anyone was down here, watching him. But he reached the bottom of the stairs without trouble.

Next came the tricky part—he had to go up the stairs. No more cover. He'd be in plain sight the whole time. The metal steps would rattle, drawing attention to him. He could be picked off with a single shot.

He took his gun out and moved up facing the main floor, ready to fire back if anyone took aim at him. Maybe he could keep them pinned down until he reached the top. But he made it all the way, walking backward, without anyone taking a shot at him.

Okay. That had to mean there were no lookouts on the lower level. If there were, they wouldn't have let him get this far, not when taking him out would have been a piece of cake.

So far, so good. But the next step was even more difficult—sneaking by a wall of office windows that stretched from floor to ceiling and left no place to hide as he made his way to the door.

Anybody in the office would see him as soon as they looked this way.

He stole toward the windows and stopped as soon as he reached glass. He poked his head out a little to see what waited for him inside the room.

Overturned office furniture and stacked-up file cabinets cut the office space in two. He could see behind them through the gaps, could see part of a television set in the far corner, a mattress on the floor and naked bodies entwined in the act of lovemaking.

He blinked. Okay, that was unexpected. *Awkward*.

But also lucky.

He could make it across the walkway, passing in front of all those windows, without being seen. Nobody was paying the slightest attention to him.

He twisted the doorknob. Locked, which he'd kind of expected. But it was a simple office door lock and he had it picked in a flat minute.

Heck, a secretary with a hairpin could have done it.

He moved inside silently and kept down as he inched forward, using file cabinet for cover. Any noise his boots made was covered by some moaning and a lot of heavy breathing, not to mention the TV running a Mexican soap opera and a fan that was going somewhere behind the pile of furniture.

The scent of sex hung in the air, which made him think of Deputy Sheriff Bree Tridle, for some reason.

He pushed her out of his mind as he pulled his backup weapon and stepped forward with a gun in each hand. "Freeze!"

The woman screamed and scampered off her man in a panicked rush, nearly kicking him in the head as she grabbed for the sheet to cover herself.

Jamie's eyes were on the guy. "Freeze! Hands in the air!"

Rico was in his early twenties, covered in gang tattoos, his gaze rapidly clearing as he grabbed for the handgun next to the mattress. He wasn't concerned with modesty.

Jamie shot at the gun and the force of the bullet kicked the weapon out of reach. Rico went for a switchblade that had been hidden under his pillow, apparently. He was nothing if not prepared.

He lunged toward Jamie.

"No! *Mi amor?*" the woman screamed, scampering farther away from them, looking shocked and horrified at the scene unfolding in front of her.

Jamie deflected the knife and knocked Rico back. "I don't want to have to shoot you, dammit!"

That slowed the guy down a little. "You no come to kill us?" He held the blade in front of him, ready for another go.

Jamie kept his gaze above neck level. "Customs and Border Protection. I'm here to talk about the smuggling your gang is involved in. You look like a nice couple. Nobody has to die today."

Wow, he was getting downright soft here.

He sounded almost as optimistic as the deputy sheriff.

Rico didn't look convinced. "Her brother didn't send you?"

Jamie stashed his backup gun into the front of his waistband, then reached for his CBP badge and held it up. "I'm only here for information, man."

Rico raised his knife and his chin, sneering with contempt. "I don't talk to pigs."

"That's generally a good policy. Snitches don't live long in this business." Jamie glanced for a split second at the young woman who was white with fear, pulling her clothes on with jerky movements, and he did some quick thinking. "But it looks to me like you have something to live for. What if you two could get away both from your gang and your father?"

"Mi amor?" The woman's gaze flew to Rico, hope mixing with alarm in her voice.

"Can't be done." Rico reached for his jeans, didn't bother with underwear. He was tough enough to rough it, seemed to be the message.

Since he wasn't sneering anymore, Jamie took that as a good sign. "A chance at true love, the two of you together. What's that worth?"

Rico considered him through narrowed eyes. "You let Maria go. Right now."

"Okay," Jamie agreed, as a gesture of good

faith. Maria probably had zero useful information for him, anyway. He looked at the woman. "Go."

She cast a questioning glance at Rico, who repeated the order in Spanish and explained that he would find her later, but she stubbornly shook her head.

A rapid argument followed before she finally ran for the door. They could hear her footsteps on the metal walkway, then down the stairs.

"I could kill you now," Rico said, still holding the knife, a nasty-looking piece that had probably seen plenty of business on San Antonio's backstreets.

"You could try," Jamie answered calmly, feet apart, stance ready. He actually preferred Maria out of the way. No sense of her getting in the middle of this and maybe being killed.

Rico measured him up again. Swore in Spanish. "What the hell do you want from me?" he asked at last.

"I'm looking for a man called Coyote."

"Don't know him." But the corner of his left eye jumped.

"Any information would help. All I need is a link I could follow to him."

"And if I give you this, me and Maria go to witness protection?"

He nodded.

"Where?"

"Someplace where nobody can find you. You can get rid of the tattoos. They'll hook you up with a job and a place to live. You can get married."

Rico still hesitated.

"Ask yourself this," Jamie gestured at the ratty, messed-up room with his free hand. "Is this the life you want for your children? Or do you want something better? Doesn't she deserve more than this?"

God help him, he was appealing to true love. Something he wasn't even sure he believed in. But maybe Rico did, and that would be enough to settle matters here.

The man lowered his knife and filled his lungs, his ink-covered shoulders dropping as he exhaled. He looked pretty damn young with all the bluster gone out of him. He barely looked twenty. "There's no way out for guys like me."

"There is now. This must be your lucky day."

Tension-filled silence stretched between them.

"Okay," Rico said. "Let me think. I might be able to get something for you. If you can keep us safe. Maria the most."

An opening. "I'll talk to my people. But I need a solid lead."

More silence, then, "How do I find you?"

Jamie reached into his back pocket, pulled out a business card with his number on it and tossed it on the mattress between them.

Rico didn't move to pick it up. He'd do that when he was alone.

"Don't wait too long to call," Jamie warned. "I found you once, I will find you again. If I have to track you down, I'll be coming to bring you in." Then he backed away, gun still in hand.

He didn't relax until he was down the stairs and out of the building.

Damn, he hoped this would get them results. Because otherwise he would have to explain to Ryder why he wasn't taking Rico back to the interrogation room with him.

He'd just taken a hell of a gamble.

BREE WAS HEADING back to her office with her first cup of coffee of the morning, thinking about the talk she was giving at the middle school later about crime prevention, when Jamie Cassidy strolled into the Pebble Creek police station.

"I'm armed and I'm not handing my weapon over," he advised Lena by the metal detector, looking as surly and aggravated and sexy as ever. He took off his cowboy hat and ran his fingers through his hair to straighten it.

"Let him through," Bree called out before Lena could tackle him.

Or something. The officer had that dreamy-eyed look again that said she wouldn't mind seeing Jamie Cassidy on his back. There were probably a million women out there who shared the sentiment, although today he looked somewhat worse for wear.

Bruises and cuts marred the right side of his face—looked like he'd taken a beating since Bree had last seen him. Given his attitude and general disposition, she could see how a person would be tempted.

She flashed him her "this is my station and I'm the boss here" look, but when she spoke, she kept things cordial. "Mr. Cassidy. Nice to see you again. Why don't we talk in my office?"

"Jamie." He strode in past her, his mouth set in a line that was suspiciously close to a snarl.

A part of her that was apparently easily distracted wondered what it would take to make him happy. Not that she was volunteering for the job. Not even if those sharp eyes and those sculpted lips of his could have tempted a saint.

She closed the door behind them. "Please, take a seat. How can I help you today?"

He lowered his impressive frame into the

nearest chair as he gave a soft growl of warning that he probably meant to sound threatening.

She found it kind of sexy, heaven help her. "Are you all right? What happened to your face?"

"Somebody whacked me."

"While the rest of us can only dream," she said sweetly. "Life is nothing but unfair." She set her mug down. "Came to share information?"

"Came for my equipment."

"Heavy-duty stuff." She didn't want him to leave until she got at least *something* out of him, so she grabbed the first-aid kit from the bookshelf on the back wall and went to stand in front of him, half sitting on her desk. "Let me see this. Look up, please."

He did, but only to send her a death glare. "I'm fine."

"Of course you are, mucho macho and all that. Which is how I know you won't be scared of a little sting."

He'd cleaned and disinfected his injuries from the looks of it; the smaller scrapes were already scabbed over, but she didn't like the larger gash over his cheekbone where his skin had split.

"I assume you didn't go get stiches because you don't have the time, not because you're scared of the needle?"

He shot her a dark look. He did that so well. Must have been part of his training.

"Why don't I slap on some butterfly bandages, as long as we're both here. Then you won't have to go see a doc. You'll save a ton of time that you can use to glare at people. I'd hate to see you slip off schedule."

His eyes remained stoic, but the corner of his sculpted mouth twitched. "Make it quick."

"How about you tell me who you guys are for real? Who do you really work for?"

"That's on a need-to-know basis."

"You're in my town, on my turf. I need to know."

"I don't think you have the right clearance, Deputy Sheriff."

He said *deputy sheriff* as a slur, as if he was calling her *babe* or maybe some other word that started with a *b*.

She focused on the disinfecting and the butterfly bandages to keep herself from engaging in contact unbecoming a police officer. When he was good to go, she closed her kit and walked back behind her desk.

"How about you tell me the basics," she suggested. "Something to get started with."

"I'm here for my equipment," he repeated.

Okay, then. He wasn't going to be an easy nut to crack.

She shoved aside a manila envelope some-body had left on her desk and folded her hands in front of her. "Just so we're clear on this one thing, this is my town. You make trouble here and I'll know why."

Being a Southern belle and a lady came nat-urally to her. She'd been raised on the beauty-queen circuit, but some days she did have her lapses. Looked like it was going to be one of those days.

His eyebrow slid higher. "Do I look like trou-ble?"

"Double serving. With whipped cream and cherry on top."

A bark of laughter escaped him, softening his face, and she caught a glimpse of what he might have been at one time, without all the darkness he was now carrying. It took her breath away.

Phew, all righty, then. She shook her head to clear the image.

So unfair that she would find him attractive. He was in her town doing secret things. He was about as pleasant as a wild boar with a tooth-ache. He was high-handed. She didn't want to like him, not even a little.

"What's your team really doing on the bor-der?" she asked again, and waited.

And waited.

"Ryder McKay said that you'll be my liaison.

Liaise." She raised her eyebrows into her best schoolmarm look.

He still waited another couple of stubborn seconds before he finally said, "We're here about the smuggling."

"But not to make policy recommendations," she guessed.

He shook his head, watched her, measured her up again. "We're here to intercept a special transfer."

"And you work for Homeland Security?"

He just stared at her.

So, okay, she could pretty much guess the rest. Whatever his team had come for probably had something to do with terrorism. "Is my town safe?"

"Yes."

"And you know this how?"

"We have *some* information. You're not a target."

Made *some* sense. Terrorists would be going for one of the major cities.

Anger coursed through her. She was a patriot and a Texan, sick of people who tried to mess with her country. "Is there anything I can help with?"

He hesitated for a moment. "Maybe. I'll let you know if we come across something where we could use your assistance."

"And you'll let me know of any developments?"

He hesitated longer this time, but said, "Yes."

"Thank you." She pulled out the bottom drawer that was about filled to the rim with his weaponry and one by one set them on the desk between them, grabbing an old canvas bag from under the desk and dropping it on top. "I'd appreciate it if you carried that loot out of here concealed."

He gave a brief nod and stepped forward to pack up his things. The string on his night-vision goggles caught on her manila envelope. They reached for it at the same time, their fingers touching.

She barely had time to register the zing as she jerked back, the contents of the envelope spilling all over her desk.

She stared at the photos for a disjointed moment as her brain registered the images: snapshots of her in her kitchen, taken from outside her house. She grabbed for them, but not fast enough.

He snatched up the last one and took a good look at it before holding it up for her. "What the hell is this?"

The photo showed her standing in her bedroom next to the bed, changing, wearing nothing but a skimpy bra and blue jeans, holding her favorite checkered shirt.

She grabbed the picture from him as her heart sped suddenly. *Oh, God. Not again.* She so didn't have time for her past to rise up to claim her. "That's on a need-to-know basis."

HE DIDN'T LIKE the way she suddenly paled, or the idea that she had a stalker.

"When do you think these were taken?" Jamie asked.

She didn't think about it long. "Last night. That's the shirt I was wearing yesterday."

"And you went to see Ryder McKay earlier in the day?" He gave her a pointed look.

"The two have nothing to do with each other."

The hell they didn't. "Smuggling is a multibillion-dollar business. It's a dangerous business."

"Really? I must have been sitting behind my desk, filing my nails, and I missed that briefing," she said with that overly sweet smile he'd come to learn meant she was mocking him.

He shot her a look that told her he wasn't amused. "Look, people around here know we're investigating smuggling. Someone saw you visiting the office. They didn't like it. You need to stay out of what we're doing."

"I'll take the risk."

"I'm not asking. I'm telling you. Don't involve yourself. Forget everything we've talked about earlier."

"Or what?" A laugh escaped her and trilled along his nerve endings. "You'll spank me? For heaven's sake. I'm an officer of the law. I'm trained to handle myself."

The visual of the spanking bit left him both speechless and breathless for a second.

"I'm a big girl, Jamie." She switched to dead serious and ticked off in a split second, which did nothing to lessen the wave of lust that threatened to drown him. "Whatever threat is jeopardizing the peace of this town and the law, you can be sure I'll be out there fighting it." She pressed her full lips together.

He wondered what she'd do if he tried to kiss her. Throw him against the wall again? His pulse quickened.

On the other hand, as unpredictable and unreasonable as she was, she might just shoot him.

Not that kissing those lips wouldn't be worth the risk, he decided. Not that he was going to do it. No way. He was in town on serious business. And women were no longer part of his life, anyway. He had too much baggage, too many nightmares. He had no right to bring that into a relationship and mess up somebody else's life along with his.

He didn't have much left. He was a trained killing machine, that was about it. He planned on living the rest of his life using what skills he had in the service of his country.

"Stick to speeding tickets," he said as he stood. "Forget about me and my team." Although he was pretty sure he wasn't going to be able to forget about her. He was going to try, anyway, he promised himself as he walked away from her.

His shift was starting in half an hour.

He walked out of the station to his SUV parked up front. At least he'd gotten a possible lead in San Antonio.

He would have to figure out the witness-protection thing with the U.S. Marshals Service. And Rico had to think about what he had and come up with enough that would buy him two witness-protection tickets.

Jamie needed to talk to Ryder about that. And forget about Bree. He would. After he made sure she was safe.

Chapter Four

Stick to speeding tickets, Jamie Cassidy had said. He had a singular ability to get under her skin, Bree thought as she went about her business.

She didn't have to worry about speeding tickets, as it turned out. Just as she finished her crime-prevention presentation at the middle school, the town's streetlight system went down, snarling traffic, cars barely inching along. She spent most of the rest of her shift cleaning up the mess.

A dozen fender benders got tempers flaring; a couple of arguments ended in fistfights before it was all over. Bree didn't have too much time to think about Jamie Cassidy, and thank God for that, because the man was enough to raise any sane woman's blood pressure.

She was exhausted by the time she made it back to the station, and then a whole other hour went to waste with writing up reports. She'd just finished when Hank, the contractor whose company managed the town's traffic-control system, walked into her office.

"Hey, Bree." He was short and round, the mocha-skinned version of Danny DeVito, a family guy who was always hustling, always working on something, if not for his kids and small company then for the town. He was a tireless volunteer.

"Everything up and running?"

"Almost. I wanted to talk to you about something." He stopped in front of her desk. "Looks like several of our control boxes were shorted out on purpose."

She stilled. "Are you sure?" Why on earth would somebody want to do that? "Can you give me the locations?"

He rattled off the crossroads and she wrote them down. "I'll look into it. Thanks for letting me know. Can I get you a coffee from the break room?" The least she could do. She appreciated the work Hank did and the fact that he took the time to come in to talk to her.

"Lena already fixed me up with coffee and a Danish." He patted his round belly with a quick grin. "I better get going. I still have a couple of things to fix."

She gave him a parting wave. "Thanks. I really appreciate it. Give me a call if you run into any trouble."

"Will do. Say hi to Katie for me," he said as he left her to her work.

She shrugged into her harness and slipped her weapon into her holster as she stood and scanned the major intersections on her list. Several stores in those spots would have external security cameras. She needed to check the footage.

Most of the officers were out on calls and the station was close to deserted.

"I'm off to look into the traffic-light business," she called to Lena on her way out. "Back in an hour, I hope. Want anything?"

"A hot guy with an oil claim on his ranch?"

"If I see one, I'll send him your way."

The traffic was clearing up at last so she didn't have any trouble reaching the first address, just three blocks from the station. The owner of the small pawnshop handed over his security video without insisting on a warrant. Bree had cut him a break a month or so ago when he'd taken in stolen merchandise without knowing.

She moved on to the next address, a place that sold used video games and gaming equipment, and got the recording there, too. She'd been buying Katie games there for years. She knew her community and was nice to people. And they were nice to her when she needed something.

The next place after that was a specialty shop, selling high-end, artisan cowboy boots, run by one of her old schoolmates.

Rounding up the half-dozen recordings took a little over an hour, including taking some time to talk with people. She liked knowing what was going on in her town.

Then it was back to the office to view the footage. Another half an hour passed before she had her men, two twenty-somethings from Hullett—Jeremy and Josh Harding, brothers. She knew them from a round-up brawl that had sent six men to the E.R. last year.

She headed out to Hullett to pick up the boys. She let them sweat it out in the back of her police cruiser—didn't start questioning them until they were in the interview room.

They both wore scuffed boots and jeans and identical ragged T-shirts, no brand, cheapest stuff money could buy. They looked down on their luck. If they were going to commit a crime, why not one that would benefit them financially? Try as she might, she couldn't figure out the traffic-light angle.

"Little old for pranks, aren't you?"

Jeremy shot a meaningful look at his younger

brother before looking back at her. "Dunno what you talkin' about."

"What do you Hullett boys have against Pebble Creek these days?" They had an arson investigation going, the fire started by someone just like these two, last week. Then there were the half-dozen cases of random vandalism she couldn't tie to anyone. Investigations that kept her busy, like she needed extra work with smuggling and the counterfeit money coming in.

"You're messing up my crime-rate statistics," she told them, putting away her softer side. "I don't like it."

The younger one, Josh, brightened. "We are?" He sounded a little too eager. Even pleased.

She looked from him to Jeremy. "Okay. What's going on here?"

"We have an alibi. We were at a friend's house, hangin' out and shootin' beer cans," the older brother said, smug as anything.

"Is that so?" she asked calmly. "Because I have half a dozen security tape recordings showing you two messing with the traffic-light control boxes."

The younger brother paled. "I can't go to no jail. Jenny's gonna have a kid. Ma's gonna skin me alive if I get into trouble again. She said it."

"Shut up, idiot," Jeremy barked at him.

Bree raised a placating hand. "How about we start with cooperation, then discuss restitution? Things don't have to come to jail."

"Sounds good, ma'am," Josh hurried to say, all manners, suddenly.

His older brother whacked him on the shoulder. "You don't even know what it means."

"Can't be worse than jail."

Bree shook her head. "It means you two have to pay back the repair costs, and then never cause trouble in my town again." She thought that was a fair deal, but Josh's shoulders sagged.

"We ain't got no money. That's why we did it in the first place," he whined, earning another smack from Jeremy.

They were only about ten years younger than she was, but she felt like she should ground them or something. "No more hitting." She held up a warning finger. "Now, explain to me how you make money from stopping traffic?"

They looked down. Looked at each other.

She pulled out her cell phone. "How about I just call your mother?"

"The mill," Josh blurted out, then slumped as Jeremy shot him a dark look that said, "I'll make you regret this later."

"The wire mill?" Hullett had a wire mill. She failed to understand what Pebble Creek traffic had to do with it.

"It's going under," Josh explained.

Not a surprise. The owner was in prison for human trafficking. A shame for the workers and their families. The Hullett wire mill was the town's largest employer.

"You two work there?"

Jeremy pressed his lips together and sulked, but Josh responded. "We already got our pink slips."

Bad timing with the baby coming, she thought. "I'm still waiting on how this connects to traffic."

"Word is, there's gonna be a paper mill comin' in. Choice is between Hullett and Pebble Creek."

She knew about that. Some rich Chinese guy, Yo Tee, who owned a big paper mill on the other side of the border, was thinking about building a smaller one over here. Probably to get a tax break or whatever. He had some team that was scouting for a location. She'd run into them the week before when an overeager citizen spotted them at an abandoned factory and reported it as a possible burglary.

"We want the paper jobs in Hullett," Josh told her. "They could put new machines into the wire mill and keep the workers on. We could do trainin'. We ain't stupid."

Clearly. She narrowed her eyes at him. "So

you're making a mess of my town to make Hullett look better. Is that it?"

He looked down at his hands sheepishly. "We need the work."

They went about it in a completely wrong and idiotic way, but she could certainly understand their motivation. "What else?"

Josh looked up, confusion on his face.

"What else have you done?" she clarified.

"The lights were it. I swear."

He looked earnest enough that she believed him. But she would bet good money that Pebble Creek's recent troubles with vandalism had been caused by some of his buddies—bunch of geniuses.

She told them she'd take them to holding, one at a time, while she figured something out. She took Jeremy first, then Josh. With Josh, she swung by the break room on their way to holding.

He walked with his head hanging. "Just don't call my ma, all right? She can't pay no bail."

"Want some coffee?"

He looked up with surprise. He'd probably expected chastisement. "Thank you, ma'am. I would."

"How about something to go with it?" She gestured toward the box of doughnuts on the counter.

"For real?"

"I'm not here to abuse people whose biggest crime is wanting to work."

Relief filled his face as he cautiously reached into the white paper box for an apple fritter.

She drew a slow breath. "But you and your brother did go about it the wrong way. Replacing those fuse boxes will cost a mint."

Josh looked like the first bite got stuck in his throat. "I told you, we ain't got no money."

"And the baby's coming," she said with sympathy. "I'll talk to the judge. You could be booked and released today, no bail. I could put in a strong recommendation for community service only. You and your brother could work off the damage." She paused. "Thing is, if I'm that nice, I need to know everything you know."

But instead of giving her information on other recent vandalism in Pebble Creek like she'd expected, he said, "I know about the bad money they were talkin' about on TV." He looked around nervously.

Pay dirt.

She hurried to the door and closed it, all ears. "Sit." She put the whole doughnut box in front of him.

But he looked really scared now, just holding on to his fritter. "If anyone finds out…"

"Not from me. I promise."

He swallowed hard and looked to the door as if to make sure nobody was coming in. "I was at Ronny's house last week for some grillin' and beer." He paused.

"Ronny who?"

"Brown. Down by the reservoir."

She knew Ronald Brown. They were old friends. She'd arrested him on drug distribution last year. He'd gotten off on a technicality. "How is he linked to the fake money?"

"I don't know. I swear." Josh put his free hand to his chest. "I went into the house to take a leak. He was in the kitchen with this other dude. The other guy was givin' him a roll of twenties and tellin' him they needed to be spent slowly and carefully."

"That's it?"

He nodded. "I didn't think nothin' of it until they said about bad money on the news."

"What did the other man look like?"

"Mexican. Short and scruffy. He had some tattoos. Ain't never seen him around before."

"How about you look at some pictures for me?"

She led him back to her office then had him look through the mug shots on her computer.

Scrolling through the pictures, and doing a lot of handholding so Josh wouldn't renege on his promise to help, took some time. By the time they ran out of mug shots to look at and she'd processed then released the brothers, her shift was over. Too late to go and see Ronny Brown. She put away her files. Tomorrow was another day. Right now, she had to go pick up Katie.

The drive over took less than ten minutes.

"Did you have a good day?" Bree asked when they were in the car, heading home.

Katie worked at a facility that employed handicapped people. They shipped small machine parts all over the country and were responsible for wrapping and packaging. The people running the place were fantastic with the employees. Katie loved going to work since all her friends were there. They had fun together.

"Mrs. Mimms said I did good work," Katie said. "I think she was happy. She made the happy face."

They'd been working on emotions with cue cards and internet pictures in the evenings. Katie was high functioning, but she did have autism. She had trouble with emotions, both displaying them appropriately and telling the mood of others.

"I'm sure she was very happy. Did you have a good lunch?"

Food was a touchy subject. Katie only liked

a handful of things, and she wouldn't eat at all if the food on her plate was touching.

"Chicken fingers. Good."

Bree relaxed a little. It worried her when Katie skipped meals. She was such a skinny little thing already.

"We got someone new," her sister informed her. "He's just like me. Except he doesn't talk to anyone. His name is Scott."

"Do you like him?"

"He's quiet."

Which meant she liked him. She gave a full report on the way home, then went through her coming-home routine, putting her things away, washing her hands, setting the table, while Bree made some hamburgers for dinner.

"Can we do a puzzle later?"

"Sure." Bree pulled the French fries from the oven—baked to save some calories—and thought how much she liked their evenings together. Katie was sweet and gentle, and part of her life irrevocably.

She didn't care if the few boyfriends she'd had over the years couldn't deal with that. They'd wanted her, but they hadn't wanted her "baggage," as the last one had put it. Thing was, she would rather have her sister than a jerk in her life, anyway. She *had* said that. With a Southern-belle smile on her face.

Still, the good things in her life far out-weighed the bad.

She thought of the pictures in the manila envelope, the first time she'd allowed herself to think of them since she'd gotten them away from Jamie Cassidy.

Trouble was coming again.

Just thinking about that made her tired.

Why now?

She would end it for good this time, she promised herself. She wasn't going to let this touch Katie, put her in danger.

As she turned to put the food on the table, movement outside caught her eye.

Did someone just step behind her garage?

She set the fries on the table. "I'm going to put the garbage out, then we can eat."

"Okay," Katie called back, cheerful and oblivious to danger, which was the way Bree meant to keep things.

She bagged up the garbage. Then she slipped her service revolver into her waistband before she walked outside through the back to confront her past that was rising up once again to claim her.

Chapter Five

Her mother's oversize garden sculptures populated the backyard, same as the front, their shapes too familiar to look eerie, even in the twilight. Bree opened the door without a sound and ducked to the right, into the warm evening air and the cover of the bushes. And then recognized the man standing by the shed—Jamie Cassidy.

You have got to be kidding me. She ground her teeth together.

She nearly sprung up to yell at him. But maybe teaching him a lesson would be a more productive way to prevent him from spying on her again. So she kept down, skulked around the rock garden and snuck up behind him, using the statues as cover.

She didn't have much in the backyard as far as tall plants went, just a few butterfly bushes, with more color added by generous clumps of black-eyed Susans and asters that were putting on quite a show of yellow and purple this fall.

She moved as silently as a copperhead, raising her gun when she was but a step behind him, anticipating the jolt he'd give when she pressed the cold metal against the back of his skull. That ought to take the cocky bastard down a peg.

Except when she was an inch away, he said, "Hey, Deputy," and reached back at the same time, clamped his fingers over her wrist and shoved her against the side of the shed, holding her hand above her head, their faces inches from each other.

His cheekbone had turned purple since she'd last seen him. He still wore her butterfly bandages. And he still looked too handsome by half. *Deal with it.* She normally wasn't a shallow person.

"What are you doing at my house?" She shoved against him with her free hand but he wouldn't budge. "I could have shot you."

"I didn't think you were the type to shoot a fellow law enforcement drone."

"How did you know I recognized you?"

"You never took the safety off your weapon."

Dismay and aggravation tightened her jaw. He'd probably seen her and tracked her movements from the moment she'd come outside.

She didn't often get caught off guard. That Jamie Cassidy had had her back against the wall twice now in the space of a week aggravated the living daylights out of her. "What are you doing here?" She repeated the question he still hadn't answered.

"Trying to catch whoever took those pictures. I think this might be connected to your visit to Ryder. Someone doesn't want you to share your local expertise with my team. Whoever is trying to mess with you might be just the guy we're looking for."

"You're just trying to scare me off so I don't stick my nose into your team's business."

"One can dream," he said lightly.

"Maybe *you* sent the pictures to intimidate me," she said, although she knew that wasn't the case.

He leaned another inch closer. His sharp gaze raked her face. "When I want to scare someone, I'm a lot more direct about it. I don't leave them guessing."

His powerful body completely blocked any escape, his fingers holding her right hand above her head as effectively as handcuffs. He wasn't trying to look threatening, she didn't think. The words had been said straight-faced, yet alarm tingled down her spine nonetheless.

Okay, and a little bit of lust, too. She didn't

think he was going to harm her. He could have done so already, countless times if that was his intention. The twinge of attraction she felt was a pure evolutionary response of a female to a display of power from the alpha male.

So unfair.

She tried to resist the magnetic field that drew her to him.

The faint scent of his soap tickled her nose, mixed with some barely there, understated aftershave. She could almost swear she could smell the testosterone coming off him, he was so ridiculously male.

He had a warrior's body, a warrior's stance, a warrior's eyes. And definitely a warrior's strength. She tried to pull away and failed once again.

"You're trespassing," she pointed out, a little testiness mixing with the twinges of lust she didn't appreciate.

He opened his mouth to respond, but Katie appearing at the back door stopped him short. He let Bree's hand go immediately and she moved out of the shadows while he disappeared into them. She appreciated that tremendously. She didn't want him upsetting Katie.

"We're having dinner," Katie said. "It's dinnertime."

"Yes, it is, sweetie. I'm coming." She hurried

toward her sister. Having her schedule interrupted could send Katie off-kilter for the rest of the evening. Better to keep everything running smoothly.

She glanced back from the doorway one last time, but Jamie Cassidy had disappeared completely.

She wasn't enough of an optimist to think permanently.

JAMIE WENT AROUND the back of Bree Tridle's modest two-story home. He'd gone off and grabbed something to eat, then came back. This time her upstairs lights were all out; there was just one light on downstairs, in her kitchen. He knocked quietly on the back door before trying the doorknob. Unlocked.

"Bree?" He didn't want to get shot.

"In here."

He moved down the dark hallway and came out into the kitchen, bathed in light. The space was plain and spotless, Mexican tile floor, simple pine cabinets. A handful of small, crystal unicorns hung in the window.

She sat at the kitchen table, a bottle of beer and a bottle of strawberry wine cooler in front of her. Looked like she'd been expecting him.

"How did you know I'd come back?" he asked as he sat, taking the beer.

"You don't look like the type who walks away without getting what he came for."

He leaned back in his chair. "I like smart women. I'm glad we understand each other."

"Let's not get carried away." She drank straight from the bottle.

Good. He didn't have the patience for prissy women. She was trying his patience in so many ways already, the last thing he needed was for her to start putting on airs.

"So why are you here, exactly?" she asked.

"I need that envelope." He should have taken it when he'd been in her office. He'd been distracted. By her. That wasn't going to happen again. He was here on a mission.

"Why would you think I brought it home? Things like that are entered into evidence."

He watched her for a long second. "You strike me as the kind of woman who would handle her personal business herself."

"I'm glad you understand that it *is* personal. I'll take care of it."

She said that with a little too much confidence. He watched her for a moment. "So you know who your stalker is?"

She shifted in her seat, reaching for her bottle again, saying nothing.

Okay, she did know. "Has this happened before?"

She gave a reluctant nod. "Back when I was competing."

Beauty pageants, she meant. She looked different now from the super made-up, big-hair pictures he'd found on the internet. She was still beautiful without a doubt, but in a hometown-girl kind of way.

She wore her hair in a simple ponytail, the blond her natural color, he was pretty sure, little makeup, dressed plain and comfortable. The kind of woman who could dazzle the hell out of a guy yet somehow make him comfortable when sitting with her. And could probably beat the stuffing out of him if he got fresh with her.

"Want to tell me about it?" he asked.

"If it gets you out of my hair."

He promised nothing. Not about keeping out of her hair, or her pants, for that matter. There was a part of him, getting louder and louder, that wanted to keep his options open.

"When I was doing the pageants," she said after a minute, her expression turning sober, "I had a young fan, Lilly Tanner, who wanted to be just like me. She wrote me several times, and I wrote back. We even met. Her room was apparently covered with my posters. She wore T-shirts with my picture on them."

She paused to draw a slow breath. "She was bullied in school and ridiculed. They called her ugly, and worse. A lot worse. Just really mean and nasty stuff." She folded her hands on her lap. "She ended up committing suicide."

"And one of her friends blamed you for it."

"Her twin brother, Jason. He's not—" she paused "—he doesn't always understand what he's doing. He was born with some mental disability and the added depression pushed him off balance after Lilly's death."

Not a comforting thought. "You need to make him stop before this escalates."

"I know." She took a drink. "I called his parents while I was waiting for you to show. They don't know where he is. He moved away from home six months ago and only keeps in touch sporadically. I'll find him."

She didn't seem scared or upset as much as sad.

"You feel some responsibility for the sister," he guessed. "The parents lost their daughter and you don't want to be the one to put their son in prison."

"Maybe." She glanced toward the stairs. "I met him before. He wasn't some evil kid. He just didn't know how to relate to the world around him."

"I don't think you're taking this seriously enough."

"We'll just have to agree to disagree."

That little crease in her bottom lip kept drawing his gaze. He looked up into her eyes. "I don't do that when I'm right."

She raised an eyebrow. "Are you ever wrong?"

"Not that I can remember."

He got the quick laugh from her that he'd been aiming for. He hadn't liked the darkness on her face, the idea that she would carry the guilt over the girl's death. She had nothing to do with that. Her happy, peppy personality might have annoyed him before, but it looked good on her. She needed to go back to that.

If anyone had a past to feel guilty about, it was him. An entire family had been killed because of him: husband, wife, four kids. He pushed away the memories, rubbed the ache in his knees, even if there was nothing there but metal.

"I like modesty in a man," she observed, irony in her tone.

He almost asked what else she liked in a man, but decided he'd better not. He needed to focus on the business at hand. "I'm going to need that envelope."

Her forehead pulled into an annoyed frown. "I know who sent it. I said I'll take care of it."

"I still need our lab to confirm whether any prints on the envelope really belong to your old stalker. Once I know this has nothing to do with my job, I'll cross it off my to-do list and you can handle it any way you want to."

"I don't need your permission to do that." But she got up and walked to the kitchen counter and pulled out an evidence bag with the manila envelope inside it. She grabbed a plastic bag from the counter, carefully transferred the photos into that and kept them. She gave him the envelope only.

He didn't feel like arguing with her for the rest. He took the bag and walked to the door. "I'll be in touch."

"Phone is good," she said.

He lifted an eyebrow as he looked back at her. "Why, it's almost as if you didn't like me, Deputy Sheriff," he said as he left her standing in her kitchen.

He walked across her small front yard, where she had almost as many garden statues as she did in the back, mostly unicorns and angels. He wondered what the story behind those was, but he couldn't wonder for long. His phone interrupted.

Rico Marquez.

"Made up your mind?" Jamie asked as he got into his car.

"Yeah, man. I got something."

"I'm on my way. Same place as before?"

"At the chop shop across the road. Come in through the back."

He hung up, then sent a text to Ryder to let him know where he'd gone. At this time of the evening there wouldn't be much traffic on the roads, but it'd still be well past midnight before he made it to San Antonio and back.

He had plenty of time to think on his way into the city. Mostly he thought about whether the meeting was a trap. But no matter which way he turned it in his head, he didn't see what reason Rico would have for taking him out. Unless his whole plea was bogus and he wanted a high-score kill to get a promotion within his gang. A possibility.

Yet the chance that he did have something on the Coyote and he was willing to share it was worth the risk. So Jamie made sure his weapons were checked and ready and that he was wearing his bulletproof vest before he pulled into the dark alley behind the chop shop and got out, sending his exact location to his team first, as insurance.

He got out of the car slowly. When he didn't immediately get hit from one of the windows, he counted that as a good sign.

The rusty steel door opened before he could knock, and Rico gestured for him to hurry inside. The lights were off in the main bay, and the smell of motor oil hung in the air. Rico led him to the office in the back but only turned on the small desk lamp there. It barely illuminated the room. The cavernous shop stretched in darkness on the other side of the glass partition.

Rico scratched his tattoo-covered neck. Pretty much every part of him that was visible was inked, including the backs of his hands. "Anyone follow you here?"

Jamie shook his head.

"You wired?"

Jamie pulled up his shirt.

Rico's glance caught on the gun first, tucked into the waistband, before he raised his gaze to scan the rest. That they would both be armed had been understood from the beginning.

Jamie dropped his clothes back into place. "What do you have?"

Rico rubbed his fingers over his mouth. "If this checks out, I get protection? For both of us? "

"That's the deal."

The man shifted from one foot to the other. "You said you're looking for the Coyote. What for? He's bad news, man."

"Let that be my problem."

Rico measured him up. A couple of seconds passed in silence.

"Last year I was in the can," he said at last, then drew a long breath. "Enrique led the gang then. He wanted to move some of our guys down south, take over. Wanted to control both sides. He wanted to be king."

"So?" Gangs looking to expand weren't exactly big news. "Where does the Coyote come in?"

"In prison, the man in the cell next to me worked for the Coyote."

Jamie leaned forward and listened.

"He wanted revenge. The Coyote killed his brother. He said he'd pass information to Enrique, help Enrique take territory from the Coyote."

"Did he?"

"He got stabbed the next day." He banged his fist against his chest several times to demonstrate. "The guards never figured out who stabbed him, but I know. A guy called Jimenez. On the Coyote's orders."

"Where is Jimenez now?"

"Nobody knows. He went underground when he got out. Might be he was killed."

Another dead end. But there was something else here. Orders got delivered through visitors. All he had to do to find the Coyote's messenger was search the visitor records at the prison, see who'd come to visit Jimenez just before the murder. Then the messenger could lead him to the Coyote himself.

"So when do we get out?" Rico asked. "I don't want to wait. Maria's ready. Tonight?"

"Give me a couple of days to finalize everything. I'll call you to let you know how and when to come in."

The thought that they would soon have a direct link to the Coyote was enough to keep Jamie awake on the drive home, no coffee needed. Even if they couldn't dig up enough evidence to charge the man with smuggling, they would have murder one if they could prove that the Coyote had ordered the execution of that man in prison. It didn't much matter under what charge the bastard was put away, as long as he was taken out of circulation.

And, most important, once they had him, they would do whatever it took to get enough information out of him to catch the terrorists they were hunting.

He thought about that, and about Bree's stalker. He didn't like the idea of Bree in danger. She was way too nice. If some bad guy came into her house she'd be more likely to offer him coffee than shoot him between the eyes.

Yet if anyone could talk her way out of a situation with smiles and politeness, it was her. He didn't fully understand how she did what she did, but he had to admit it worked.

That was a whole different approach from how he operated. He'd been trained to identify the enemy, aim, shoot and kill. She needed someone like that to back her up, just in case.

Not that he was volunteering.

He just wanted to make sure her stalker wasn't connected to her recent cooperation agreement with his team. He hoped she was right. He hoped it was something else, a misguided regular Joe, like she'd said, and not some professional criminal sent to harass her.

He had work to do and she was a distraction. He wanted to figure out what was going on so he could close the door on the whole business and walk away from her. As soon as possible.

Chapter Six

She'd planned on going out and finding Ronny Brown to ask him about the suspicious roll of twenties Josh had seen him receiving, but by the time Bree dropped off Katie at work and got to the office the morning after Jamie's surprise visit to her house, she had a visitor waiting. The CIA had sent an agent in response to her call about the fake twenties.

He was a full head taller than she, clean shaven, blond hair cropped, black suit crisp. He carried a black leather briefcase and wore the exact kind of CIA sunglasses actors wore on TV. He had a strong jaw, straight nose, good build.

Hot, Lena mouthed from behind him, grinning. Looked like she wouldn't have been against a full-body search if the opportunity presented itself. Not that she was a lecher or anything, or someone who flitted from guy to guy. She just had a cheerful personality and

a zest for life, and she noticed and appreciated pretty things and hot guys and whatever
else made life good to live. She fostered rescue
puppies and went skydiving on the weekends.
Working with her was fun, because she was
fun, and because she was also an extremely
competent officer.

Sexy, she mouthed next with a wink.

Not as sexy as Jamie Cassidy, Bree thought.
Not that she was here to check out men. Or
that she was interested in either of them. But
she wasn't blind. Especially to Jamie, whose
dark gaze had managed to haunt her dreams
all night, damn him.

The visitor nodded at her. "Deputy Sheriff."

"You must be Agent Herrera." She shoved
Jamie out of her mind and returned the agent's
smile as she showed him into her office. Since
he was already holding a disposable cup he'd
probably picked up at a drive-through, she
didn't offer him coffee. "Why don't you take
a seat?"

She turned on her computer, then unlocked
her top drawer and extracted the three evidence
bags that held the three twenty-dollar bills
she'd seized so far. "I have time and date, and
the circumstances of how and where the bills
were obtained, including names and contact
information."

"I appreciate it. It's always good to work with competent people." The agent held one of the bags up to the light and examined the banknote.

"Can you tell anything just by looking at it?"

"Just that it's pretty good quality. We'll have to run some tests. Could be leftover from an old batch we've already seized."

She thought about Ronny Brown, the clue Josh had given her. What had Josh seen in that kitchen? Somebody handing over a roll of bills. Ronny hadn't been caught with any fake money, and most vendors in town were checking. She'd put the word out right after the first case.

More likely than not, the money Ronny had received had to do with drugs. That was his usual speed. She would check him out before she said anything to Agent Herrera and look like a small-town rookie, too eager to jump the gun. The agent wouldn't appreciate having his time wasted.

And she didn't need to look like a fool just before sheriff elections. Not that she was running. Being sheriff took more time than she could give. First and foremost, she wanted to be there for Katie. But the new sheriff would be her boss, and she didn't want his first impression to be that she was an imbecile.

"You find a lot of counterfeit money?" she asked the man.

"Not that much. But when we do, we take it seriously. Out of every ten thousand dollars in circulation, about three are fake."

He glanced through the window of her office at Lena, who caught the look and smiled at him. The agent's gaze lingered.

Well, what do you know? "Will you be staying?"

"For the rest of the week." He laid his briefcase on his knees, opened it then carefully placed the three evidence bags on top of some papers before looking across the desk. "If I need a place to interview people?"

"Feel free to use our facilities." Lena could show him around.

"Thank you, Deputy." He stood. "I'll be in touch." He pulled a card from his suit pocket and set it on her desk. "If you come across any information that might be relevant to this case, I'd appreciate it if you'd let me know."

"Of course."

He left with a parting nod.

Okay, definitely handsome, if a little dry for her taste. But Lena was a big girl and had the right to pick her own poison, Bree thought with a smile as she stood to go for coffee.

The corner of a manila envelope in her in-box caught her gaze.

Her stomach clenched.

So stupid. Now she was going to be scared of envelopes? It could be anything.

But she used her shirtsleeve to carefully tug the envelope from the pile. Unmarked, it was the same size and color as the one the photos had come in. Lumpy. *Not pictures this time.*

She stepped over to close her door, then pulled two rubber gloves from the box in her drawer and put them on before she opened the clasp.

Visual first. She peered inside and could see some kind of fabric. Dark. She carefully tilted the envelope, holding it by the corners until the contents dropped onto her desk.

Black lace panties, she registered a split second before recognizing them as hers.

Jason had been in her house. Anger and concern pulsed through her in alternating bursts, her teeth clenching.

He was getting braver. Of course, he was nine years older now—no longer the adolescent kid she remembered, but a man.

When her phone rang, she picked it up without looking at the display, her attention still on the slip of black cloth in front of her. She eased it back into the envelope in case someone came in, while balancing the phone between her shoulder and ear. "Bree."

"Just wanted to make sure you got to work fine and everything's okay," Jamie said on the other end.

Because an arrogant outsider keeping tabs on her was what she really needed. He was on some superteam. If he thought just because she was a small-town deputy and a woman she was clueless, he had another think coming. She didn't need his "protection."

"Thanks for the concern, Mr. Cassidy." She exaggerated her Texas drawl. "I might have strained my pinky, holding it out while I was sipping tea. Also, my corset pinches a little, but other than that I'm okay."

A moment of heavy silence passed. "Don't mock me." Then another pause. "And don't talk to me about corsets."

The deep timbre of his voice as he said that sent a not-altogether-unpleasant tingle down her spine. She was as bad as Lena out there with Agent Hottie. Uh-uh, not going to happen. She didn't even like Jamie Cassidy. And she had way too much going on to get tangled with a man right now.

She filled her lungs. "Is there a particular reason you're wasting my time this morning?

Did your team find anything you'd like to share with me?"

"Any new contact from the stalker?"

She shoved the envelope into her top drawer. "No." She didn't want or need Jamie Cassidy's help. He was too much of a distraction.

"You hesitated."

She rolled her eyes, even though she knew he couldn't see it. "My stalker is my problem."

"Not until I'm sure he's not coming after you because you got involved with my team."

He was like a dog with a bone. She closed her eyes for a second. "He's not. I told you."

"We'll see when the envelope comes back from the lab. I'm on border patrol today. I'll stop by tonight to talk about whatever happened since I last saw you."

"Nothing happened."

"Put another beer in the fridge for me," he said before he hung up on her.

She was an upbeat person normally. She really was. But Jamie Cassidy was getting on her last nerve. If he showed up at her house tonight, they were going to have to have a serious talk about boundaries.

She was *not* going to let him keep on distracting her. She drew a deep breath and refocused on her work, then walked out of her office to check with Lena about a bail-bond issue they hadn't yet resolved from the previous week. Then she would track down Ronny Brown.

Lena was just hanging up the phone when Bree exited her office. "Discharge of a firearm at the Yellow Armadillo," she said in a "what else is new" tone.

"Bail-bond agent come in yet?"

"All taken care of."

"I'll see about the Armadillo." And off Bree went, without her morning coffee.

Traffic was light, the sky a clear blue, yet tension stiffened her shoulders. Jason was going to be trouble. And Jamie Cassidy... Not thinking of him on her drive over to the bar was more difficult than she'd anticipated. Those eyes and that fallen-angel face...

She was normally pretty good at self-control. The fact that he was rapidly getting under her skin aggravated her more than a little. She put all that away when she reached the Yellow Armadillo.

She found about two dozen guys wasting away their lives inside the dingy space when she walked in with her weapon drawn. She focused on Ronny Brown, who was standing in a group of three people in front of the bar. Okay, so maybe her day was turning for the better.

Except for the small problem that two of the men had their guns drawn.

"Just the guy I want to see," she told Ronny in her calmest tone. He was the only one in the group who was unarmed, and he looked less than happy about that, his gaze darting around as he tried to find a way out of his predicament.

She flashed them all her best smile. "Gentlemen, what seems to be the problem here?"

A young Mexican guy with gang tattoos she hadn't seen before was pointing his gun at Ronny. Both their lips were bleeding. Shorty, the bartender, a grizzly ex-oil-rig worker who stood over six feet tall, was holding the mother of all rifles on them, keeping them in check.

"How about we all put our weapons down? Just as a matter of common courtesy." She was trying to set a good example by lowering her own.

Tattooed Guy swore and swung his gun to point at her then squeezed off a shot. As she ducked, not shooting back since there were people all over the bar, the bartender squeezed the trigger on his rifle. The boom made glasses rattle all over the tables and her ears ring.

But instead of hitting Tattooed Guy, Shorty somehow ended up shooting Ronny, who must have gotten in the way. Ronny went down screaming. A light hit in the leg, nonfatal, Bree registered, yelling, "Somebody call 911!" as Tattooed Guy ran for the back door.

"Keep Ronny here." She threw the words at the apologetic-looking bartender, as she took off after the gangbanger. "And, for heaven's sake, nobody shoot anyone else," she called back as she ran. "I mean it!"

She burst through the back door into a narrow alley between rows of buildings, into a wall of heat and the stench of garbage. The place hadn't grown any more pleasant since the last time she'd made a bust back here.

Tattooed Guy was dashing forward a hundred yards ahead of her, somewhat encumbered by pants that had been below his waist earlier but now were slipping lower. Not the first time she was grateful for the stupid pants-on-the-ground fashion. It was definitely a boon for law enforcement.

"Stop! Police! Drop your weapon!"

Instead, he shot back over his shoulder.

The bullet slammed into the wall next to Bree, sending wood slivers spraying. She felt a sharp sting at her neck but didn't bother to check. Injuries would have to wait until later.

Feet set apart, she braced both hands on her weapon. *Aim. Shoot. Bang.*

She took the shot without emotion, the only way to do it—no aggravation now, no anger, nothing but the job. The man sprawled onto the gravel face-first, sliding another foot or two, carried by his momentum. He was going to leave some skin behind, she thought as she ran forward.

She'd hit him on the back of his right arm. Blood leaked from the sleeve of his T-shirt. But he pushed himself up, ready to run again.

Too late. She was on top of him by then.

"You have the right to remain silent," she started, and kept on going with his rights as she tied his hands behind his back, ignoring his moaning and complaining, yanking him up just as he progressed to threats.

Fortunately for him, she was a good enough shot to have caused only a light injury. Unfortunately for her, that meant he was well enough to dish out a heap of verbal abuse.

"Hey! Is that any way to talk to a lady? You kiss your mother with that mouth?" She had a badge and she had a gun. She didn't need to take sass from anybody.

She got him back to the bar but pretty much had to shove him the whole way. The bartender still had Ronny at gunpoint. Ronny sat on the floor, pale and looking as if he was in shock, holding his bloody thigh with both hands.

She looked around at the patrons, most of whom had gone back to drinking and talking, although they were keeping an eye on her and the proceedings. "Anybody else hurt?" she called out.

"Nah."

"No, ma'am."

The replies were all negative.

She shoved Tattooed Guy onto a chair and made sure he wasn't bleeding heavily enough to bleed out before the ambulance got there. Then she hauled Ronny up and cuffed him before letting him drop back down to the floor.

She glanced over her shoulder. "Dammit, Shorty, put that rifle away. I got this. They're not going to cause any more trouble." She searched the men's pockets and dropped the contents into separate evidence bags: money, bullets, cigarettes. The stranger was Angel Rivera, according to his driver's license.

She turned back to the rest of the patrons when she was done. "All right, cowboys, start lining up for your witness statements."

She called Lena, then took statements painstakingly, had each person sign theirs, not that she got much out of them. Ronny and Angel had apparently been sharing a drink in one of the more secluded booths when they'd started arguing. Then Angel had fired a shot at Ronny before Shorty took matters into his own hands and restored the peace.

Lena arrived at about the same time as the ambulance. Bree let her take over Shorty and the witnesses while she went to the hospital with the two men.

She started grilling them while waiting for the E.R. doc. No sense in wasting time. There'd be a dozen new things waiting for her when she got back to the office. Crime didn't take a break just because she got busy.

She started with Ronny. "Want to tell me what that was about?"

The man shrugged.

"The Angel guy looks like bad news to me. He disliked you enough to take a shot at you. And that was before. Now he's going to the can for it. How much you think he's going to like you when he comes out?"

Ronny stayed silent.

"Looks like a gangbanger to me. You know his type. They come with a lot of close friends, and revenge is their middle name."

Ronny was beginning to look nervous, squirming on the bed—a good start. A little more motivation and he would probably break.

"I don't like outsiders coming into my town, causing trouble," she said, hinting that she was willing to take Ronny's side on this.

That seemed to help.

"He says I owe him money," Ronny said at

last, then swore colorfully and at length. "Lyin' bastard. I ain't owe him nuthin'."

"Where is he from? I haven't seen him around here. His tattoos don't look familiar." She knew most of the gang tattoos for the groups that were active in her county.

"San Antonio."

"I don't like it," she said, half to herself, half to the man. San Antonio gangs moving down this way was the kind of trouble she didn't need. "Are you getting into something over your head, Ronny?"

His shoulders sagged, his expression turning miserable. "My leg hurts."

"I know. They'll look at you in a minute." She patted his arm. "Look, I got enough problems already. CIA's here, pain in the neck. They're investigating all that counterfeit money business. I got my hands full. How about we clear this up right fast and we all go our own way?"

His gaze cut to hers, panic crossing his face. "CIA's investigatin' here? In Pebble Creek, you mean?"

"Yeah." She shrugged. "They take counterfeiting seriously. Thing is, you've kind of been implicated. I've been looking for you, actually."

He cast a desperate glance around, opened his mouth, closed it, opened it again. "I have nothin' to do with it, I swear."

She nodded. "Then none of the bills I took off you will have any trouble going through the scanner? You know I'm going to have to check them."

He froze, panic written all over him. Then Angel cleared his throat on the other side of the green divider and Ronny caught himself, sat up a little straighter in the propped-up bed. "I don't know anything about that."

"I have an eyewitness."

He closed his eyes and grimaced, then, after a moment of hesitation, lifted his hands, palms out. "It was all Angel, I swear," he said, obviously having come to a decision. He was more scared of the CIA than his gangbanger associates, apparently.

Something rustled on the other side of the green divider hanging from the ceiling. "Shut up," Angel called over, his tone plenty threatening.

"I'll get to you, Mr. Rivera. You just hang in there," she told the man and made sure she didn't turn her back to him.

He could try to grab her—even with one hand cuffed to the bed—if he was stupid enough to go for it.

She made sure she was ready for anything as she tried a few more tricks with Ronny, but he really did seem to be clueless. He got the bills from Rivera, and that was all the information he had.

When she was done with him, Bree pulled the divider open and stepped over to the other bed. "How about you continue the story? Ronny got the money from you. How did you come by it? You just took a shot at me. That's assaulting a police officer. You want to be very helpful now." She waited.

"No hablo inglés."

"Yo hablo español. See? It's your lucky day." She flashed him her nicest smile, even though she didn't feel like it.

But Angel just stared daggers at her and wouldn't answer any questions no matter what language she asked them in or what she promised or threatened. If looks could kill, she would have been lying at the foot of the bed in a sticky, red puddle.

She kept on until the doctor finally showed up to check on the men. While he did that, she stepped outside and called the CIA agent to fill him in. Now that Ronny had confirmed a connection to the fake money, she had something solid to pass on to the agent.

She might not have gotten a ton of information, but they were one step closer to the source of the bad money. Progress.

Agent Herrera could come and see if he

might get further with the two dimwits if he felt like it. She also called Delancy to stay with Rivera until the man could be taken into custody. She needed to get back to the office and take care of other business.

BORDER PATROL WAS a bust: no movement all day. Jamie used some of the time to call the lab to check on Bree's envelope. Several times. They had a partial print, too smudged to be of much use, but they were trying to digitally enhance it before running it through all the databases again.

At least he made some progress with setting up witness protection for Rico Marquez and his girlfriend, calling around to make sure all the pieces were in place for a problem-free extraction.

He could have left it to the U.S. Marshals Service; they ran the program just fine. But he'd given Rico a promise, so he made sure he kept an eye on the process and was part of the decisions. He sure hoped Rico would have something usable for him in exchange.

When his shift was over, Jamie swung by his apartment—a utilitarian, sparsely furnished space he basically only used for sleeping—took a shower and changed before heading over to Bree's place. He checked the perimeter first.

She kept her property tidy, as did the rest of her neighbors. Seemed like a nice, family kind of neighborhood. She should have been safe enough here.

When he was sure all was clear and nobody suspicious was hanging around, he walked up to the front door and knocked.

"I should have locked you up for that fake twenty and all those weapons," she said as the door opened. "Just to keep you out of my hair."

She wore a pink T-shirt with jean shorts, her long shapely legs making his mouth go dry as they caught his attention, his brain barely registering the words she was saying. Then he blinked and caught up.

"You think of me and you think of handcuffs?" He wanted to see her off balance for once. "A man could take that as encouragement."

But she just burst out laughing.

She was way too cheerful by half. Thing was, he kind of liked it. He'd lived in darkness for so long, she felt like sunshine on his face.

As she lifted her chin, he caught sight of a bandage on her neck and his whole body went still, his protective instincts plowing forth like a steam engine. "Are you hurt?"

She raised a perfect eyebrow. "Chill. Just a scrape. The bullet didn't even hit me."

He didn't like the thought of a bullet anywhere near her. He wanted to ask how it'd happened, but he was interrupted.

"Who is that?" came a call from somewhere in the house.

He had thought they would be alone, that her sister would be asleep by now.

"That's Katie, my sister. She stays up late to watch her favorite shows on Fridays." Bree eyed him with hesitation.

He had no doubt she wanted to kick him out. But she was too much of a lady to do it—the beauty of Southern hospitality.

"It's been a long day." He piled it on. "Hot out there on that border. I sure could use a cold drink."

Her sister stepped into the foyer and stopped, her eyes fixed on Jamie. She looked a lot like Bree in her coloring but shorter and slighter. She wore jeans and a T-shirt with a pink unicorn in the middle.

"Katie, this is Jamie, a friend from work," Bree said.

"Are you a police officer?" She watched him without blinking, as if she had X-ray vision.

"Kind of," Jamie answered. "How are you, Katie? Nice to meet you."

"I'm watching my show," she said after some

time, then padded away, barefooted on the Mexican terracotta tile.

"She likes you," Bree said, a frown smoothing out on her forehead. "If she didn't trust you, she would have stood there until you left to make sure you were out of our space."

He followed her into the kitchen, spacing out a time or two when his gaze slipped below her waist. Those shorts should be illegal. Then again, she was wearing them in the privacy of her home. He was the idiot for coming here and asking for trouble.

Katie paid little attention to them, sprawled on the rug on the living room floor in front of the TV, watching some crime show as intently as if she was memorizing every word.

Bree brought him a cold beer, along with a glass of orange juice for herself as they sat down, the same as before.

She caught his gaze on Katie. "Autism. She's very high functioning. She really doesn't need a lot of help," she said with a proud, loving glance toward her sister, not as someone who was bitter or embarrassed. "She's as good as you and I in a lot of things, and in some things she's better."

He wouldn't doubt it. "You're lucky to have each other."

She tilted her head, her shoulders relaxing.

"Most people say she's lucky to have me." She watched him for a second or two. "They don't know anything."

"I have seven brothers and a sister."

She muttered something that sounded like, "God help the women of the world," under her breath.

He added a silent amen. His brothers were... His gaze slipped to her legs. With a view like that, who could think about his brothers?

"Seven brothers and a sister," she repeated, sounding more awed than snarky this time around. "That must be great."

It was, even if he'd spent the past couple of years pushing his family away. He'd been in a dark mood after he'd come back from Afghanistan without his legs.

"We have our moments."

He didn't ask if she was from a big family. He'd read her file. She only had Katie. Her parents had both passed away a decade ago in a house fire. He glanced at Katie, who was watching her show, completely mesmerized. "You're close."

Part of him envied that connection. He'd had that before. And he couldn't blame anyone for losing it. He'd been the one to push his family away.

"That's the best part of having a sister." She was smiling, but a shadow crossed her eyes.

"And you would want to keep her safe." He came around to the purpose of his visit. "So if there was anything strange going on, you'd tell me."

She straightened in her chair. "I don't need your protection. Seriously, Jamie, you're handsome and all, have that whole warrior thing going, but we have to stop meeting like this."

She thought he was handsome? That tangled up his thought process for a few seconds. "Where would you like to meet?" A certain part of him was voting for her bedroom.

"On the phone when you call to update me on what your team is doing in my town," she said deadpan.

She was a tough nut to crack. Good thing he didn't mind a challenge. "How about your case? Any progress with the counterfeit money?"

"The CIA is here." She gave a small shrug. "I caught two guys today who are connected. One doesn't know anything, the other one isn't talking."

His gaze slipped to her neck again, the muscles in his face tightening as he reached out and touched the edge of the bandage for a second before drawing back. "You had a tough day. Might as well tell me about it. Chances are, if I get what I came for, I'll leave faster. I want to know about what's going on with your stalker."

She rolled her eyes at him. But then her face grew somber as she thought a little before saying, "I got another envelope today."

His body tensed as he watched her closely. "More pictures?"

She shook her head. "Something more personal. He took something from the house this time."

His fingers tightened on the cold bottle. "He's escalating. He came in. He's getting closer."

"I don't think he'll make contact. He didn't before."

Which meant absolutely nothing. "What did he take?"

"None of your business."

He had to ask. "Anything that could be considered sexual?"

She nodded with reluctance.

Anger cut through him. "You know what that usually means in cases like this. He wants you and he hates you at the same time. It's not a good combination."

"I know. I thought about that. He was an adolescent boy the first time he became obsessed with me. Now he's all grown-up."

He turned that over in his head a couple of

times, considering the implications. "Why come back now, after all these years?"

"He's been living with his parents until recently. He took off without notice. I'm guessing he stopped taking his meds."

More bad news. "What if he pushes even closer?"

"I'm a trained officer of the law. I'm always armed. Katie is never home alone. If I have to go back to the office for something, Eleanor, our neighbor, comes over. And Jason is not after Katie, anyway. He's after me. He just wants to scare me and have a good laugh about it. He gets off on showing how clever he is."

"You're sure it's Jason Tanner?"

"Pretty sure."

He hoped so. A messed-up average Joe would be easier to handle than if the smugglers, ruthless killers, were coming after her.

"You got the envelope for me?"

She got up and brought it to him with a resigned shake of her head.

"Whatever he took is still inside?"

"Not a chance, buster."

Of course, the more secretive she was, the more his imagination tortured him. He watched her from across the table, held her gaze. There were enough sparks between them to set her kitchen on fire.

He wasn't sure what to do with all that heat. He'd never wanted anyone with this intensity before. He would have liked to think he had enough self-control to not cross certain lines, but the hell of it was, he wasn't sure.

"I'm not relationship material," he said, just so they understood each other. If anything were to happen, he wanted her to be fore-warned.

She flashed him an amused look. "Good thing I'm not looking for a boyfriend. I'm not looking for a man at all, in fact." She tilted her head. "Your being here is more like harassment than a date. We're clear on that, right?"

"I don't want you to be upset."

"Because you don't want to be my boyfriend? I think I'll live."

"I meant if we end up sleeping together."

She was just taking a sip of her juice, which she coughed up, some of it through her nose. She grabbed for a napkin and dabbed her face, then wiped the droplets of juice off the table. "You think we're going to sleep together?" She looked at him, bewildered.

She'd never looked sexier.

"I'm pretty sure," he said miserably, with all the resentment he felt. She was the one who'd barged into his life at that bookstore. He hadn't asked for any of this.

"No."

"Okay." He nodded. "That's good." He didn't need that kind of grief.

BRIANNA TRIDLE, THE most beautiful woman in the world, had a guy in her house.

The man watching her from the outside didn't like that. His hands tightened on his camera as he observed through the kitchen window, hidden in the darkness. Clouds covered the moon, and he'd picked a good spot, wedged between two tall bushes. He was good at hiding. He was good at a lot of things. He didn't care if people called him stupid.

Brianna was inside in the light. She was pretty. He wanted more pictures of her. He liked looking at her. He always had. But he didn't want pictures of her with the other man.

She belonged to him. She was supposed to be waiting for him. He'd come back to forgive her. But she was betraying him.

Rage washed over him so hard it had him grinding his teeth.

The doctor said he had to control his rage. The doctor said a lot of things. He didn't like the doctor. He wanted to do what he wanted to do, and not what other people told him.

Chapter Seven

Tracking down Jimenez—Jamie's one lead to the Coyote—proved to be a difficult task. He'd been released from prison two months before, unfortunately, current location unknown. Jamie was running down leads all day, calling Jimenez's family and dropping in on his known associates, trying to get a bead on him.

Nobody knew where he was or, if they did, they weren't telling. He drove back to the office in a bad mood, which didn't improve when the first thing he heard was, "Why the long face? Deputy Hot Chick slapped the cuffs on you again?"

Shep grinned at him from behind his computer. "She can do a full-body search on me anytime she wants," he finished.

"Beauty Queen Babe?" Keith joined in, coming from the back with his coffee. "Oh, man. She's a walking fantasy.

"Watch it before you get lovebug fever," Shep shot at Keith. "It's going around in the office."

He wasn't lying. Ryder and Mo, two guys as tough as they came, had recently been bitten.

"You look at a woman too long, next thing you know you're shopping for a ring," Shep warned Keith, the youngest man on the team.

"Not me, old man," Keith vowed as he plopped into his chair. "Spending your life with one person is like...medieval. Who does that anymore?"

Keith had a playboy side. He was young and full of energy, and had the looks to pull it off. Jamie had seen women walk up to him and hand over their phone numbers on more than one occasion when they'd been in town together, running down leads.

Not that Jamie'd had any trouble in that department, either, before. He'd meant to get married. Coming from a big Irish family, marriage and kids had always been the assumption, the expectation, even. He'd been in love, or he'd thought he'd been. He'd been on the verge of getting engaged.

Then he'd come home without his legs and given Lauren her freedom back. She hadn't protested. And her leaving hadn't destroyed him.

He hadn't been seriously interested in anyone else until now. Good thing he and Bree had been able to clear the air between them. There was some attraction, fine, but neither of them wanted to see where it might lead.

They both had other things to do. They both content with the way things were. Big relief.

He booted up his laptop and let Shep and Keith argue over the merits of serial dating. He tuned them out when he saw that he'd been emailed the prison visitors' log for the day he'd requested. Since he couldn't find Jimenez, he had to figure out who carried the hit order to him from the Coyote.

But as he opened and scrolled through the file, he soon realized that the logs weren't overly helpful. Jimenez had had two visitors on the morning of the day when he'd killed the inmate who'd been about to betray the Coyote.

Neither of the visitors were fellow gang members, but a priest with a prison reach-out program, and Jimenez's girlfriend, Suzanna Sanchez. Jamie checked the address given in the log—San Antonio—looked up the phone number online and made the call.

"I'd like to talk to Suzanna," he said when the line was picked up on the other end.

"Wrong number." The male voice sounded elderly.

He confirmed the address and was assured

he'd gotten that right. And after a few moments of conversation, it became apparent that he was calling an apartment building where tenants rotated in and out on a regular basis.

He thanked the man and hung up, entered Suzanna's full name and last known address as well as approximate age into the most comprehensive law enforcement database he had access to. He had a new address and new phone number within seconds. As luck would have it, she was living farther south now, less than twenty miles from Pebble Creek.

This time he hit the jackpot.

"I need to talk to you about your boyfriend, Jimenez, ma'am."

"You found the bastard, ay? You gonna make him pay child support now?" She misunderstood him.

He didn't correct her assumption. "Could I stop by so we could talk in person?"

"*Sí.* I'm at home. Where else would I be? He left me with three *niños.* I can't afford no daycare to go work no more." She went on cursing Jimenez both in English and Spanish.

Keith was still trying to convince Shep of the beauty of open relationships. Jamie tracked down information about Jimenez's other visitor, the priest, via the internet, grabbed his address, too, then took off to see Suzanna.

She lived in an immigrant neighborhood where people ran into their houses when they saw Jamie's truck roll down the street. They were afraid of immigration. He slapped his fake CBP badge on. Better if they think he was here checking on her immigration status than if they thought she was snitching on her old boyfriend to law enforcement. Jimenez was a hard-core gang member. His buddies wouldn't take well to traitors.

He checked his gun before he got out, then walked to the patched-up trailer that looked like it was on its last legs; the roof was repaired with corrugated steel, the siding was missing in patches. One good storm and the thing would collapse. He didn't like the idea of little kids living in a place like that.

When he knocked, a young woman in her early twenties came to the door with a baby on her hip and two toddlers clinging to her legs. She wore thrift-store clothes, nothing but suspicion on her face.

Her gaze slid to his badge.

"I'm green-card citizen," she said. "My children all born here."

"May I come in, ma'am?"

She stepped aside to let him in and closed the door behind them. She didn't ask him to sit. "You said you wanted to talk about loco bastard Jimenez."

"When was the last time you saw him?"

"In the spring. I went to visit him in prison. Told him I needed money for the *niños*."

"Was that all you discussed?"

"He said he give me money when he free. But he never came here when he got out, not even a once." Frustration tightened her voice, tears flooding her eyes. "He's no good *hombre*. You see him, you tell him I want to put knife in his heart."

The anger seemed sincere. "Did anyone ask you to take him a message?"

"No, *nada*. He no family here. His mother lives in Mexico. His brothers all shot dead." She crossed herself.

"How about his friends?"

She rolled her eyes. "He no let me meet no friends. He's jealous man. He hit me if mailman brings package to door. He wants me to him only. Much love before." She shook her head. "Now he want me no more."

He stayed for another twenty minutes, asking what she knew about Jimenez's job, his friends, the people the man hung out with. He asked about messages in prison again, but she knew nothing and he believed her. She didn't seem like a seasoned criminal, just a woman on the edge after making too many bad choices.

Jamie ran the information he had so far through his head as he walked to his car. Jimenez executed one of the Coyote's men in prison, one who'd been on the brink of betraying the Coyote. Jimenez was one of the Coyote's men, but couldn't be found. If Jamie caught the messenger who took him the hit order, that guy could lead him to the Coyote instead.

Jimenez's girlfriend didn't pan out. Jamie drove up to see the priest at the mission next, which was nothing but an abandoned pizza store in a strip mall.

The front windows were busted, possibly shot out, now patched up with cardboard. Father Gonzales, an older man sitting inside, sported a blue sling, but his face immediately stretched into a smile as Jamie walked in.

Jamie introduced himself then gestured at the windows with his head. "Rough neighborhood?"

"We do gang rescue," the sixty-something priest said. "The gangs don't like it. The Lord's work is not always all puppies and rainbows, I'm afraid."

The priest seemed to have a good sense of humor about it, even if sitting in a storefront unarmed while ticking off some of the most ruthless criminals in the state didn't seem like a smart plan to Jamie. He kept his opinion to himself. He asked about Jimenez instead.

The priest remembered him. "A troubled young man. Yet so much to live for. All things can be forgiven."

"Did you try to convince him to leave his gang? Is that what you were talking about when you went to visit him in prison?"

"That and Jesus. You'd be surprised how many of these young men wear the cross. I try to convince them to live by its principles. We talked about that and his children's future."

"Do you keep in touch? Have you talked to him since his release?"

"No." He sounded genuinely saddened. "I'm afraid I wasn't good enough. We might have lost him. But the Lord doesn't give up on anyone. And neither will I."

"You might be fighting a losing battle, padre."

But the old man smiled with full conviction. "That cannot be. It's too important a battle to lose. There are thirty thousand gangs in this country, did you know that? Eight hundred thousand gang members. Do you know what the life expectancy is for these young men?" He paused for a second before he went on. "Twenty years. Just enough to leave some orphans behind."

The sad truth. "Jimenez has three small kids."

The priest shook his head. "I lost contact with the mother. I would have liked to help her. She moved at one point. I think paying the rent is difficult for her."

Jamie considered him. He seemed like a good guy. "I can give you their new address. They looked like they could use a little help."

He talked to the priest some more to get a better feeling for him. He definitely seemed to be the genuine article, believing in what he was doing, even willing to give up his life for the men he was trying to save. Jamie couldn't see him passing a kill order.

But then, who?

Could be the order hadn't gone straight to Jimenez. It could have gone to one of his buddies inside, then passed on to him. Who did Jimenez hang with in prison?

Rico Marquez might have the answer. And he wanted that new chance through witness protection enough to cooperate.

Jamie called him on the drive back to Pebble Creek but Rico didn't pick up his phone. He'd have to try again later.

He returned to the office just in time to go out on patrol with Shep.

"I'll meet you by the river," he told his teammate as they got into their cars. "I need to check on something first."

He wanted to drive by Bree's place to make sure everything was okay there. He tried to make a habit of doing a drive-by check every time he was passing within a few miles of her house.

Not because he liked her. She was annoyingly cheerful. She fought crime by being nice. What was that? Utter nonsense. She was a disaster waiting to happen. That was the only reason he was checking on her. *Not* because he cared or had more than a passing interest in her.

Yet his blood ran cold as he turned the corner and saw the police cruisers lining her street.

Her front yard was destroyed. Tire marks crisscrossed her rock garden, her collection of garden statues scattered around in pieces. Violence and destruction hung in the air.

He noted her car in the driveway as he came to a screeching halt and jumped out, Officer Delancy running to block his path. He was about to shove the woman out of the way when Bree appeared in the doorway.

She had a tight look on her face, her beautiful smile missing. "It's okay. You can let him pass."

He hurried to her, assessing the damage, trying to figure out what he'd missed. "What the hell happened here? Why didn't you call me?"

"Just got home. I have to get back inside. Katie is upset." She turned back in.

When he followed her, she didn't protest.

"We need to talk." They needed to have a serious discussion. Her stalker was progressing from bad to worse pretty fast. He'd gone from watcher to invader to violent attacker in the space of a few days.

Whether she wanted to admit it or not, she was in serious trouble.

BREE WATCHED AS Katie rocked herself in the living room, tears rolling down her sweet face.

"The unicorns are broken," she repeated.

The mess outside was a major disruption in her life, and she didn't deal well with disruption.

Bree wanted to give her a hug, and she could have used a hug herself, but Katie didn't like when people touched her in general, and she didn't allow anyone to touch her at all when she was upset like this.

"What can I do to help?" Jamie asked quietly behind her.

"She's—" Bree folded her arms around herself, her throat burning. "Those statues are pretty much the only thing we have left of Mom. She made her own molds. It was her hobby. She made all those unicorns because they're Katie's favorite."

She drew a slow breath and let her arms down. She needed to be strong and to take charge. They couldn't get stuck in this terrible moment. They had to keep moving forward, get past it.

"How about we get ready for dinner?" she called to Katie, trying to sound as cheerful as she possibly could. "Let's start cooking." They needed to get back to their regular schedule. The familiar chores would offer comfort.

"You need to go someplace safe," Jamie said in a low voice that only she would hear.

She'd thought about that already. "I don't know if Katie could handle that right now. She's not good with change under the best of circumstances. I asked for police protection. We should be okay here as long as we have that."

"You need something 24/7."

She shook her head. "That might be overkill, I think. Jason has done what he set out to do—he scared us. I really don't think he'll come back."

He frowned at that assessment. "And if he does?"

"I can handle things when I'm home. If I

have to go in and leave Katie with Eleanor, there'll be a cruiser sitting by the curb with an officer." Bree had responsibilities at the station. Her job didn't always conform to a nine-to-five schedule.

Jamie was watching her with worry in his eyes. "What can I do?"

She searched his face. He seemed to genuinely care. She didn't want to be touched by that, but she was, anyway. "I don't know."

"But you'll let me know?"

Why? They weren't friends. They were nothing to each other. And yet, she nodded.

"I have to go on patrol."

"Go. There's nothing you can do here right now. It's all over." She hoped.

He didn't look convinced. He left her with a dark look on his face. Through the window, she could see him check over her yard and talk to Delancy before he got into his car and drove away.

"Everything's okay," she told Katie. "We'll fix this. We always fix everything, right? We're the superteam." They'd gotten through worse, like their parents' deaths in the fire.

Yet whatever they'd faced in the past, they'd never been in physical danger.

She went to the kitchen and started preparing dinner. Regaining normalcy was the key. "How about you set the table?" she asked Katie again. They needed to get back to the mundane. She needed to settle Katie down before she could start thinking about how to solve their problems.

She wanted to be out there, securing the crime scene, taking tire casts, looking for prints and clues. But her sister would always come first.

She could hear her front door open. Probably Delancy. She called out, "Back in the kitchen."

"Just me." Her neighbor, Eleanor, shuffled into view, wearing one of those ankle-length flowery dresses she preferred. She was in her sixties, kind faced with pixie-cut hair and lots of artsy jewelry.

She always cheered Katie up, as she did now. Katie stopped rocking as soon as she saw her.

"How are you, Katie, sweetie?" Eleanor asked her.

"Somebody killed my unicorns."

"Oh, I don't think so, honey. Unicorns are magic. I bet they're just sleeping."

The distress on Katie's face didn't ease. "Magic doesn't work. It's a trick."

"Sweet mackerels, did you hear that nonsense on TV? You just wait. Unicorn magic is special." She winked, pulling a bag from behind her back. "Guess what I brought you?"

"Chocolate-covered pretzels!" Katie sounded excited at last. Then turned to Bree. "I can't eat dessert before dinner."

"That's right." Not that she wouldn't have let Katie eat absolutely anything to cheer her up, but rules were an important thing for them, something that provided Katie with stability in a world she didn't always understand.

"Here." Eleanor gave Katie the bag. "You keep this safe until after dinner. You're in charge. Somebody has to be the boss, right?"

Katie looked pleased about that.

Eleanor walked out into the kitchen. "How can I help?" she asked Bree.

"I think we're good. She's calming down. But I'm not looking forward to her going outside tomorrow morning and seeing the destruction again. She's going to Sharon's house to hang out." Sharon was Katie's oldest friend. They'd grown up together, and now they worked together.

She looked from Katie back to Eleanor. "Thank you for calling the station."

Eleanor reached a hand to her chest. "He was crazy. Shook me up." She shook her head. "Plowed right through the lawn with his big pickup. And then back and forth, back and forth. Sweet mackerels." She sank into a chair as if just thinking about it drained the strength from her. "Had to be drunk as a warthog."

"Did you see his face?"

"Young guy. I already told Officer Delancy. Honestly, I was too far away to get a good look at him. And he was turning back and forth, backing over things. Was he on drugs, do you think?"

"I don't know. But we'll definitely find him." Bree pulled a pizza from the freezer and popped it in the oven. "Why don't you stick around for a slice?"

"Don't want to be in the way." But she looked pleased as peaches at the invitation.

She lived alone, not that she was lonely. She had a flock of girlfriends and they were always off to some garage sale here or a flea market there. They had big dreams of finding something rare and making a big splash on *Antiques Roadshow.* Half of them were in love with the furniture-expert twins.

"You know we love you. And we love your company," Bree told her.

So she made the pizza, tossed a salad to go with it and they all ate together, and shared the chocolate-covered pretzels before Eleanor went home. She liked to turn in early.

Bree watched Katie's favorite prime-time crime shows with her and opened a new puzzle to keep them busy during commercial breaks. When Katie remembered the statues and got upset again, Bree gently guided her back to the picture they were putting together piece by little piece, a modern-art painting titled *Sisters*.

Not until Katie was asleep did Bree go out to Delancy. The others were gone by then, Delancy taking night shift for the protection detail. She didn't have much information, just that the forensic teams had done a good job and they should have something by the next day.

So Bree went back inside. She wanted to stay close to Katie. Sometimes, when she went to bed upset, Katie had nightmares.

Bree thought about the attack, about how serious the danger was that they were in, about what she could do if things escalated further. While she'd been telling the truth when she'd told Jamie she didn't expect this to get any worse, she was smart enough to know that it paid to have a plan B, just in case.

If they needed to go somewhere for a while... She needed to make plans ahead of time, start talking to Katie about it now, prepare her that they might be leaving. Jamie would approve. He seemed to have been genuinely worried about them.

He seemed to always be here, whether she wanted him or not. Not that long ago, she'd found that aggravating. But today, his checking up on her had felt nice, actually.

And then, since she'd thought about him just before bed, of course, she dreamed about him. In her dream, she definitely wanted him. She wasn't even surprised that he was the first person she saw in the morning when she looked out her window as she brushed her teeth.

Chapter Eight

It looked as if he'd come here straight from his shift on the border. He'd definitely been there for a while, because half the statues had been repaired and were back in one piece. The front yard no longer looked as if someone had swung a wrecking ball around. Huge, huge improvement compared to the night before. Bree couldn't believe her eyes.

She ran a brush through her hair, then checked in on Katie, who was still fast asleep. They didn't have to get up early on Saturdays since neither of them worked. She threw on a pair of jeans and her favorite red tank top, jumped into flip-flops and hurried outside.

Boy, it was getting hot already. But with Jamie there, she didn't spend much time thinking about the weather. He had a way of commanding a person's full attention.

"Thank you," she said as she reached him. He didn't have any new bruises, didn't look like he'd been in any fights last night with smugglers.

"You're messing up your lines," he said as he straightened, his clothes covered in dust. "Usually you ask me what the hell I'm doing here."

She made a face. "It's so unmanly to cling to the past like that."

And he almost smiled, which was big progress for Jamie Cassidy. He wasn't exactly the type one would expect to break out in a song and dance. Although if he did, she'd definitely watch.

"Thank you," she said again as she examined his handiwork. She could barely see the cracks. He'd fitted everything back together nearly seamlessly. There was something sexy about a man who knew how to do stuff. As far as she was concerned, competence had always been an aphrodisiac. "How do you know how to do this?"

"My grandfather was a mason, came over here from Ireland. I helped him build all kinds of things when I was a kid. He used to hire me in the summers. We worked on a couple of old churches together." He brushed a mortar-looking plop of white off his knee. Not that it made a difference. He was pretty much covered in grime.

She was a Texas country gal. Dirt never bothered her.

He wore dusty blue jeans and a black T-shirt with a sweat stain on his chest. Who knew sweat could be so sexy? Her gaze caught on his bulging biceps as he lifted a chunk of unicorn back onto its pedestal.

A decade ago, the kitchen fire that had killed her parents had taken the house. A tragic, freak accident. Katie had been on her first sleepover at Sharon's place. Bree had been away at college.

The fire marshal had said afterward that it looked like their mother had been overcome by smoke at the top of the stairs. And their father wouldn't leave the house without her. He was found with his arms around her, protecting her to the end.

The house had been the least the Tridle sisters had lost that day.

Everything had to be rebuilt, an exact same replica of the old house for Katie's sake. Bree had even replaced the furniture with similar pieces. She'd done a fair job, but it was only the statues that were part of the original property. Katie treasured them. They provided good memories and continuity.

Bree watched Jamie as he worked without

pause, his focus on the job. "This will make Katie happier than I can tell you."

"It's good to be moving a little after sitting in the car all night on patrol. I don't have to be at the office until noon. I should be able to finish here."

She was pretty sure between night patrol on the border and office duty he was supposed to squeeze some sleep in there somewhere. Yet she didn't have it in her to send him away. Having the statues fixed would mean the world to Katie.

"I'm making breakfast," she told him. "Why don't you come inside in a little while and have something with us?"

He watched her for a second. "Will Katie be okay with that?"

She smiled. "She will when she sees this."

And then she walked back toward the house, her heart a little lighter. She walked by Delancy's cruiser and thanked the bleary-eyed officer for her help, then sent her home to rest.

"Are you sure?"

"Jamie will be here for a while."

Delancy shot her a curious look.

"It's not like that," she said.

"Sure it isn't. He's obviously just a concerned bystander," Delancy said with a suddenly saucy grin, then drove away with a wave.

Bree went inside and cooked breakfast: scrambled eggs with salsa mixed in, home-style bacon and skillet cakes. She put on some coffee, too. Lord knew she needed some, and she had a feeling Jamie probably did, too.

Katie came downstairs just as Jamie was entering the house.

"You're Bree's friend," she said thoughtfully. "Your name is Jamie Cassidy."

"Yes it is. Is it okay if I visit?"

"Jamie is fixing Mom's statues," Bree told her sister, and watched as Katie ran to the window, her eyes going wide. She clapped her hands at the sight that greeted her.

Bree could barely talk her into coming to the table to have some pancakes. "Come on now, or they'll get cold and you don't like that."

That did the trick. Katie ran to the table and plopped onto her chair. "Unicorns sneeze Skittles," she said, her gaze snapping back to the window every five seconds.

"Mom used to say," Bree explained. Katie had loved unicorns for as long as she could remember. Because unicorns were different, but great. Just like Katie. Not worse than other people at all, just different and special. Her mother used to say that to her when she'd been younger and asked why some kids at school made fun of her.

There wasn't much bullying. For one, Katie's teachers simply didn't stand for it. And also because they'd had a neighbor kid at the time who was in the same grade and always stood up for her. Bree had been too many years ahead of Katie to be of much help. They had never been in the same school building together.

"Skittles come from unicorns? That's awesome." Jamie was playing along.

"Only not these ones," Katie explained with all seriousness. "Because they're made of stone. And also because unicorns are imaginary. They sneeze Skittles in our imagination. Having imagination is a good thing. And Skittles are real."

"Well, thank God for that," Jamie countered, not a trace of his dark looks and surliness in evidence.

Katie nodded as she ate. During breakfast her gaze kept straying back outside, then returning to Jamie again. They stuck to small talk, mostly Katie asking questions. She was good with questions. She wanted to know everything.

She would have made a good detective. Maybe that was why she liked crime shows. She followed a different one every night, had a TV schedule she stuck to religiously. She could usually guess the killer halfway through the story.

"What kind of car do you have?" she drilled Jamie.

He told her. "It's the blue one, out by the curb." He nodded toward the window.

Katie looked, nodded, then turned back to him. "Where do you live?"

"Are you married?"

"Do you have kids?"

"Do you have a sister?"

The questions kept coming. She was impressed with the seven-brothers-and-a-sister thing.

Then it was time for Bree to take her to Sharon's house, just a few blocks away.

Jamie was still working in her yard when she came home. He was pretty close to finishing. The improvement he'd made was amazing. With some minor cleanup on her part, the front yard would be back to normal in no time.

"I'm so grateful that you're doing this," she told him. "Katie is very impressed with you, by the way. She couldn't stop talking about you to Sharon."

He shot her a questioning look.

"Sharon is a friend from work. They hang out Saturday mornings together. We don't have a big family. I want her to have friends."

Especially since she worked for the police. She wanted Katie to have a support system if anything happened to her.

He put the last chunk of concrete in place and smoothed down whatever white cement mixture he was using to glue the pieces together. The unicorn looked fully recovered. Even jaunty. Her mother would approve, she thought out of the blue, and the thought made her smile.

"Why don't you come inside to clean up?" she offered.

He looked down on his clothes. "Okay. That might be good. Thanks. I'll just go out back and clean off these tools with the garden hose first."

She went with him, helped then they walked inside together. She led him to the sink in the laundry room and brought him a towel. "Anything interesting happen out on the border? I see nobody whacked you," she teased. "Must have been a slow night."

"It was pretty quiet," he said as he cleaned himself up, taking the jab in stride. "Every night is not a full-blown monkey circus, thank God."

She had stepped to the window when she'd shown him in, which she now regretted. The space was too small for the two of them and he blocked her way out as he peeled off his T-shirt, washed it under the water then hung it on a peg while he cleaned off his amazing upper body.

Oh, wow. He was incredibly built. And scarred. She tried not to stare, but was pretty much failing miserably. Water droplets gathered on his dark eyelashes, making them look even darker.

When he was done, he shrugged into the wet T-shirt.

"I could toss that into the dryer for you," she offered, finding her voice.

"In this heat, it'll dry as soon as I go back outside. Actually, a little cold feels nice. I don't mind. It's been a hot morning."

It was still pretty hot, as far as she was concerned.

He finger combed his wet hair back into place. "How is the counterfeit investigation going?"

"The CIA agent is doing his stuff. How about your op?" She was so proud of herself for still being able to think. She definitely deserved a pat on the back for that one.

"More dead ends than you can shake a stick at. I got a lead, kind of." He shrugged, the movement of his muscles accentuated by the wet T-shirt. "It's a long shot, but it's better than nothing."

Quit staring. Say something intelligent. Semi-

intelligent. Okay, anything that doesn't have to do with rippling muscles.

"Did I see your car up by the mission yesterday? I was up there at the tackle shop to pick out a pole for one of the officers who's retiring. Mike. We're doing a group gift. He likes fishing," she added inanely.

He watched her for a moment as he hung up the towel to dry.

Oh, right. "You probably can't say what you were doing up there."

But he came to some sort of decision, and said, "I was running down a lead on a prison hit. Someone from the outside brought the hit order during a visit. I need to find out who. Father Gonzales was on the visitor log so I checked him out. Do you know him?"

The thought of Father Gonzales being involved in any kind of criminal activity made her laugh out loud and distracted her from his body, at last. Okay, partially distracted.

"He's as antiviolence as they get. He would give his life for you, but participate in murder?" She shook her head. "No way. I've known him all my life. I'd stake my career on it that he didn't have anything to do with an ordered hit."

"Pretty much the impression I got." He nodded, frowning. "Except, here's the thing—there were only two visitors, the priest and the girlfriend. Every instinct I have says she's clean, too. So where does that leave me?"

"The message could have been transmitted through a third party. It might have gone to another inmate first, then he passed it on to the actual hit man."

"That's what I've been thinking. I need to follow up on that today. Man, that's gonna be a time killer. It's a big prison with a ton of inmates." He didn't look happy. "We don't have extra time on this."

"What does your ordered hit have to do with the border?"

"Nothing you need to worry about."

She stepped forward, her dander rising. "I thought we've been over that. Everything that happens in my county I worry about. Does this have to do with smuggling? I could help you with that. I have a pretty good grip on the usual suspects. I know the players. Look, I've been doing this for a long time before you got here."

His gaze dipped to her lips, and she realized she might be standing too close, but she didn't want to step back and have him interpret the move as her backing down.

"It's smuggling related," he said after a moment, with a good dose of reluctance.

Oh, she thought as she recalled his team's

purpose here. She narrowed her eyes. "Does this have anything to do with terrorists?"

And then he kissed her.

For a brief second, she wanted to shove him away and demand answers. And then suddenly she didn't have it in her to pull away. A small part of her knew he was probably kissing her only to distract her, but most of her didn't care.

It was sooo good. *Oh, sweet heaven.*

His lips were firm and warm on hers. She hadn't been kissed in a long time, and it'd been even longer since she'd been kissed by a guy who could make her skin tingle just by being in the same room with her.

One second it was just kind of a brushing of lips, then his mouth slanted over hers and he went for it.

Sweet mackerels, as Eleanor would say.

The heat was crazy sizzling. She wouldn't have been surprised if her hair started smoking.

Why now? Why him? He was anything but uncomplicated.

She wasn't the instant-attraction type. She didn't fall for every handsome face. She was friendly when it came to…friendship. But when things went past that… It took her forever to warm up to a guy that way.

All the instant heat now caught her by surprise. He tasted her lips, slowly, carefully, doing a thorough job of it. By the time his tongue slipped in to dance with hers, her nipples were tingling. She was helpless to do anything but open up for him. He sank into her with a soft growl that was out-of-this-world sexy.

As he tasted her fully, all her blood gathered at the V of her thighs. And he hadn't even put his hands on her yet. She was in so much trouble here.

Her head swam. Ridiculous. Deputy sheriffs didn't swoon. It had to be against regulation. Maybe the eggs she'd made for breakfast were bad. She'd rather consider food poisoning than admit that Jamie Cassidy could undo her like this.

Desire washed over her, again and again, in ever-strengthening waves. He made her want things that…

Her brain stopped. Her body took over.

Wow, okay, she missed being with a man.

HE WAS SO turned on he couldn't see straight. Lust took over his body. Testosterone flooded his brain. What few brain cells were still working were overtaken by confusion. And surprise that he could still respond to a woman like this.

He wasn't sure if he felt hopeful or resentful about his body's overwhelming response to her.

Plain and simple, she knocked him on his ass.

He wanted her now, here, hard and fast. He couldn't see beyond that.

He eyed the washer hopefully. He could lift her on top of that, wrap her endless legs around his waist. His body hardened for her. "I want you," he said in a rusty whisper as he pulled his head back a little.

"Yeah, I think I got that," she responded in a weak tone.

Her beautiful eyes were hazy with passion, turning him on even more.

He swallowed a groan. "I don't want to want you." He didn't want the complications that would come with it. He kissed her again, anyway.

It felt a lot like falling. He didn't like falling. He'd spent months falling all over his face in physical therapy after he'd gotten his new legs. Thinking of that made him think of what would come next, in a normal encounter between a man and a woman who wanted each other.

Taking off their clothes somewhere upstairs. She melted against him. Some feeling that was a lot softer and lighter than he was used to lately pulled him forward. He pulled back. She made him want things he didn't want to need.

SHE WAS BREATHING hard and hoping he wouldn't notice. *He didn't want to want her.* Well, other than the part of him that obviously did. Was it pitiful that she desperately wanted him, aching with need between her legs?

She was so damn stupid. She'd tried this before. It never worked. And it was her fault. She would always put Katie first and whatever guy was in her life would want to come first. Completely reasonable.

The kiss had been great, but she couldn't, shouldn't, go too far down this road with Jamie. The longer she let this go on, the more hurt she'd be at the end. One guy she'd fancied herself in love with had asked her to put Katie into a home so he could move in and they would have some privacy.

That had caught her off guard, broke her heart, made her feel stupid that she'd thought he was different than the others. And here she was, thinking the same again, about Jamie.

"I'm sorry. I shouldn't have done that." She shouldn't have kissed him back. "This is not going to work between us. It's not working for me."

He stared at her. Shook his head. "I apologize if I read you wrong."

He hadn't. He'd read everything right, had done everything right. She'd wanted him, wanted him still, even right now, wanted nothing more than to go back into his arms and be kissed silly all over again.

She was tempted beyond words to throw all caution to the wind and just do that, let the chips fall where they may. Except she'd done that before, and the chips always fell on heartache. She was an intelligent woman. She wasn't going to make the same mistake over and over again when it came to men.

He didn't need to know that her knees were still weak from his kiss.

Quick. Say something unaffected and clever. Not a damn thing came to mind.

Then she blurted, "Did you check both lists?"

He blinked, looking at her as if she was from another planet. "What both lists?"

"The prison keeps two separate visitors' logs. One for general visitors, the other for the attorneys and whatever. That's maintained separately. And they won't show what attorney visited what prisoner."

The heat in his eyes simmered down little by little. "That sounds stupid."

"It's to maintain attorney-client privilege," she told him, proud of herself for sounding like a professional instead of a moonstruck teenager, even if on the inside she felt more like one than she cared to admit. "Could be Jimenez's lawyer was the one who took him the hit order."

Chapter Nine

On his way home, Jamie called into the office and asked Ryder to put in a request for the new set of visitors' logs. There also had to be court records that would show who had defended Jimenez during his incarceration. They would have to jump through a couple of hoops and wait for warrants, but they could definitely get the information. *Progress in the case.*

Which was a good thing, especially since his liaison with the deputy sheriff was getting worse and worse. He was definitely going in the wrong direction with Bree. She was completely right. He'd been way off base, way out of line.

He wasn't looking for a relationship. There was absolutely no reason to stir things up with her. Good thing she had a sober head on her shoulders and saw their mistake for what it was.

He'd gotten carried away with her. It wouldn't happen again.

The kiss… He drew in a slow breath then released it as he pulled into the parking spot in front of his apartment. It wasn't going to happen again. Definitely.

Maybe she'd forget.

Maybe she barely noticed, he tried to tell himself as he drummed up the stairs. Then he swore at his own stupidity. While the kiss had been completely unprofessional, it was also utterly unforgettable.

He'd been a hairsbreadth from pushing further. Common sense, mission objective and regulation be damned, he'd wanted her, then and there, all the way. Which meant one thing: time to take a giant step back from Bree Tridle.

He showered using a plastic chair since he couldn't stand under the water, drew the blinds, went to bed. He refused to think about her or how she'd felt in his arms, but then, of course, he dreamed about her. In his dream, their interlude didn't stop with kissing. He woke a little while later in a haze of heat and lust, pulled the pillow over his face and forced himself back to sleep.

This time, his dreams turned darker. He was in the torture chamber in the hills of Afghanistan, in the cave that had been converted into a prison just for him. Outside the iron bars, enemy fighters held the family who had sheltered him after his chopper had gone down.

He was the sole survivor of his team. With two broken legs.

The first week, they tortured him to gain intelligence. He resisted. The second week, they tortured the family: husband, wife and children. He almost talked then. The third week, when the family had been reduced to bloody corpses, his tormentors had turned their attention back to Jamie once again.

They moved from hooking him up to batteries to chopping off body parts. They'd leave his tongue for last, so he could tell them what they wanted to know, they'd said. Everything else was fair game. They'd started from the bottom up.

By the time he was rescued, he was mad with pain and more than half-dead from blood loss. And a different man from the one who'd taken that chopper in.

Ex-beauty queen Brianna Tridle needed a man like him about as much as she needed a shot in the head, Jamie thought as he woke, then dressed grimly and got ready to go into the office, then out on patrol again.

He needed to pull back from Bree and keep his distance.

BREE HAD JUST gotten home with Katie when she got called into work.

"Jesse called in from the liquor store. He caught a fella with a fake bill. He's holding him at gunpoint. I can handle it if you want," Lena offered.

Bree always had the weekends off so she could be with Katie. She drew a deep breath as she thought for a second, then came to a decision. "I better go. I'm supposed to liaise with Agent Herrera on the counterfeiting." She watched Katie go into the kitchen for a snack. "I'll call Eleanor over to stay with Katie. I need someone to watch the house."

"I'm on my way."

"Thanks. I appreciate it." She hung up and called Eleanor. "Any chance you could come over for an hour or so? I have to go out on a call."

"Anytime, hon," her neighbor said on the other end. "You know how much I love that sweet girl. Spending time with her is a pleasure. I'd just be sitting home all lonesome, anyway."

"You're going to run into a good man one of these days."

"I'd take the one you had out in your front yard yesterday." She chuckled. "If you tire of him, you just send him my way."

"He's not my boyfriend or anything," she started to say, but Eleanor was already ringing the doorbell. "Okay, I'm out here."

Bree opened the door and they put away their cell phones simultaneously.

"Thank you. I really appreciate this."

"Just as long as you have cookies in the cupboard." Eleanor's sweet tooth was as bad as Katie's.

"Always."

"Hi, Katie, sweetie." The older woman walked in. "I was a little lonely tonight. Mind if I come over? I like your TV better, anyway. It's bigger."

That's how they played it lately, since Katie, twenty-three now, had been asking why she still needed a babysitter. Bree wouldn't have hurt her feelings for the world, but she wouldn't compromise her safety, either.

"I'm going to run out for a minute. You two have fun," she told her sister. "Leave me some cookies."

Eleanor walked her to the door to lock it behind her.

"Lena will be by in a few minutes," Bree said. "I just... With the vandalism thing..."

"We'll be fine," Eleanor said. "Don't you worry about us, hon." Then she added, "So about your young man?" And watched Bree speculatively.

"It's not like that. He's just a friend."

"Honey, a man puts in that kind of labor on

your front yard and he doesn't send you a bill in the mail, it's more than friendship."

"It's not the right time for me for anything more."

"You can't still be thinking that. It doesn't have to be either Katie or a man, Bree. You're so reasonable and flexible about everything else. You know what a guy like this is called?"

"Jamie?"

Eleanor gave a quick laugh. "A keeper. Think about it."

She promised nothing, but walked to her car and got in. She glanced back at the house as she waited for Lena.

She wasn't terribly worried about safety. Jason wanted *her.* If he ever escalated to the personal-attack stage, he'd be coming after her, and she could handle him.

She waited a few more minutes. Called Lena. "I'm five minutes away."

"All right. I'm going to get going here. I don't like the idea of Jesse holding anyone at gunpoint."

He was an ornery old geezer who'd had a father and grandfather in the bootlegging business. Jesse had cleaned up his act and took his status as the first upstanding citizen in his family seriously. He was way past retirement age. He claimed he'd owned his small store since before the flood. He protected his turf. He'd been known to put the fear of God into any kid who showed up for liquor with a fake ID.

She called Agent Herrera on her way over. "Got a new counterfeit bill. I'm on my way to pick it up and take a statement from the person who tried to use it."

"I'll drive over."

She gave him the address, then turned down Houston Ave.

A small crowd had gathered in front of the liquor store by the time she pulled up front, gawkers watching through the glass as Jesse kept a young, gangly guy pinned in place by the checkout counter.

"Deputy Sheriff." She flashed her badge, although most of the people there knew her. "Nothing to see here. Please, disperse." She got out of the car and strode straight to the door.

She wasn't scared. It was South Texas. Most everyone out in the country had a gun or two. Most knew how to use it. Jesse was cantankerous, but he wasn't a hothead.

"It's Bree. I'm coming in, Jesse."

She put her hand on the door handle, pushed it in an inch, then said again, "Jesse? It's Bree. I'm coming in."

"Come on in, darlin'. I got you one here."

"I appreciate it. How about you put the gun down?"

Jesse lowered his rifle. "You takin' him in?"

"You bet." To get the man away from Jesse, mostly. She turned to the younger guy. This one she didn't know. "I'm Bree Tridle, deputy sheriff. How about we go down to the station and talk about that twenty?"

"Yes, ma'am." The kid seemed mighty motivated, looking between the door and her.

"Do you have ID?"

The kid dug into his pocket and handed over his driver's license. Garret Jones, age twenty-two, lived a few towns over.

"All right, Garret, I'm going to take you in for a short interview." She looked at Jesse behind the counter and gestured toward the twenty in front of him. "Is that it?"

Jesse nodded. "Yep."

She pulled a rubber glove from her back pocket, an evidence bag from the right and bagged the money. "I appreciate the call. Go easy with the gun next time. Just a call would be fine," she added, just as Agent Herrera walked in.

He looked Garret over.

"You want him?" she offered.

"You take him in," he said. "I'll ask a few questions here, then I'll be coming in, too."

"See you later, then."

"Thank you, Deputy."

She got the kid in the back of her cruiser without trouble. He didn't say a word all the way to the station. She didn't push him, either. Agent Herrera would be questioning him, although she would ask to sit in on it. Whether counterfeiting fell under the CIA's jurisdiction or not, whatever happened in her town was her business.

Another hour, she figured. Then she'd be heading back home to Eleanor and Katie. Maybe she would take them to the mall for window shopping. They were all in need of a break.

JAMIE DROVE DOWN the deserted dirt road along the border. Everything was quiet. He'd been watching the flat expanse of arid land, keeping an eye out for the slightest movement as he talked to Shep over the radio.

"Ever been in love?" The words popped out of his mouth without warning, surprising even himself.

"Repeat that?"

"You ever been in love?"

A stretch of silence followed. "I had girlfriends."

"I mean real love."

"Hell, no. Who needs that aggravation?"

Exactly. "Come close?"

Another stretch of silence. "Kind of liked someone. Didn't work out. Bad deal all around."

"How bad?"

"She cost me my job, stole my car and set my house on fire. That's all I'm going to say about that," he added gruffly. "And I'm going to have to kill you if you ever repeat it."

"Understood," Jamie said with full sympathy, sobered more than a little. This was exactly the kind of confirmation he needed. Walking away from Bree was the right thing to do. He'd known that all along. And now Shep agreed.

His phone was buzzing. He glanced at the display. "Gotta go."

The labs at Homeland Security worked around the clock, and he'd marked his evidence "contact with results immediately." They were calling back.

"All right, give me the good news," he said.

"Both envelopes were sent by the same person. Jason Tanner."

Bree's old stalker. She was right. Better this Jason guy than the alternative. At least the mess at her house wasn't connected to the smugglers.

"Thanks." He hung up, a little relieved. Her stalker had nothing to do with the smuggling. He was free to walk away.

Except, no way was he going to be able to do that, not after kissing her, not after meeting Katie, not after seeing the destruction in her front yard.

Despite his best intentions, he'd somehow gotten tangled.

Oddly, the thought of that didn't bother him nearly as much as he'd thought it would. Bree was one of a kind. She was… All right, so he had a soft spot for her. There, he'd admitted it. Didn't mean he had to act on it. Ever again.

While that thought felt very self-righteous, it also felt incredibly depressing.

He was about to call her to let her know about the fingerprints when his police scanner came on. He caught the code first.

Fatal shooting.

Then came the address in a staticky voice, and his blood turned cold. He whipped the car around and shot down the road like a rocket, calling Shep.

"There was a shooting at Bree's place."

"Go. I can call Mo to cover for you."

"Thanks."

His car couldn't move fast enough as he flew over the uneven road, his heart thundering in his chest.

When he hit the actual paved roads and had to worry about other cars, he kept hitting the horn in warning, flying around them, putting every bit of his training to use. Then he reached her street and saw the police cars in her driveway for the second time in two days.

Caring about someone was a heart attack and a half, he decided.

He squealed to a halt and jumped out, his blood running cold as he registered the shattered living room window. He pushed his way inside, but an officer stepped in his path.

Then Officer Delancy, coming in behind him, spoke up for him. "He's with Bree."

"Where is she? Is she hurt?"

Delancy shook her head.

He could breathe again. "Katie?"

"It's the neighbor woman."

He hurried down the hallway and into the living room. An old woman lay on the floor, her chest bloodied, cops securing the crime scene.

He went in as large a circle around them as he could, ran up the stairs. "Bree?"

"In here." The words came from the back.

He caught sight of a neat master bedroom and sparkling-clean bathroom as he made his way to her, to Katie's room where Bree was sitting next to her sister on a pretty pink bed.

Katie was rocking, wide-eyed, talking too loudly. "Eleanor. Eleanor. She. She. She…"

"Shh. I know. It's okay."

Katie's gaze flew to Jamie, and the look in her pretty dark eyes broke his heart. "Eleanor is not sleeping."

"No."

"You can fix her. With unicorn magic."

"I can't, Katie. I'm sorry."

She rocked harder and moaned, ground her teeth.

He flashed a helpless look to Bree. "What happened? What can I do to help?"

She had shiny tracks on her face. She shook her head as she stood.

He walked over to her, then stopped short. He'd almost pulled her into his arms. But she didn't want that. She'd been pretty clear about it. He shoved his hands into his pockets instead. That bullet had been meant for her, he knew without a doubt, and the thought about killed him.

"I have to stay with her," she said in a low tone. "Could you go downstairs and check out what's going on? There's an address book in the top drawer of the TV stand. Could you bring that up? I want to be the one to call Eleanor's brother."

He nodded. "We're going to talk about this. It's gone too far. I'm going to upgrade your security." She might not want his kisses, but she would have his protection. He had a team. They each could spare a few hours here and there. Starting with him.

She didn't protest. A good thing, because no way was she going to talk him out of this.

"Does it hurt?" Katie asked.

Bree knew what she meant. "She's not hurting. It's not like when you cut your finger. There's no pain at all in death."

"She has blood. When I cut my finger, it bleeds and it hurts."

"Only when you're still alive."

"She's dead."

"Yes, she is, honey."

"Why?"

The question was killing her. *Jason Tanner*. It had to be him. And if he'd been the one to shoot that gun, then she'd been the target. She'd underestimated him, underestimated the danger he posed. But she wouldn't do that again. She was going to bring the little bastard in.

Sitting inside while other officers processed the destruction outside her house had been difficult the other day. Sitting up here while they processed the crime scene downstairs was nearly impossible. She was a cop, had been a cop for a long time. Everything she was pushed her to go, to hunt, to bring in the man who'd done this.

"Where did Eleanor go?" Katie asked. "The window broke and then she fell down. And then she wasn't there."

No, not in the lifeless body, Bree thought. Katie had always been very perceptive about things like that. Looked like the shooter had pulled up to the front and shot Eleanor from his car. An easy distance, and she'd been standing in a lit room.

"She went someplace else," she told her sister.

"I don't want her to go someplace else."

"Me, neither," she said and blinked back tears. "Do you want to turn on the TV?" She wanted to give her sister something else to think about. Katie wasn't good with emotions. Grief was hard for her to grapple with. It would take a long time and a lot of talking, a lot of getting used to.

"We don't watch TV now."

No. Their favorite shows weren't on until later. "Maybe we'll catch a rerun. Something good."

"Okay."

She turned on the TV and found a repeat episode of *Bones*. Katie liked that. Bree wanted to hug her sister, wanted to be hugged in return. She'd almost run into Jamie's arms earlier, would have done it, but he'd held himself so obviously aloof.

She'd been the one to push him away.

And yet, the fact that he didn't pull her into his arms still hurt. The exact kind of unreasonable female logic she always hated. She wasn't a drama queen. She was a deputy sheriff. She was strong and capable. Because she'd always had to be strong and capable for her sister.

But just now, some emotional support would have been great.

A small part of her honestly regretted pushing Jamie away.

Maybe Eleanor had been right and she saw things too much in black-and-white, at least when it came to her private life. Just because her life wasn't optimal for a long-term relationship, maybe it didn't mean that she couldn't have anything.

Except it did. Because she wasn't the one-night-stand type. When she fell for someone, she fell completely, which always ended up in heartbreak.

She'd accepted that. Accepted that she would give relationships up.

But it hadn't hurt so much until today.

Jamie popped his head in, address book in hand. He handed it over. "Why don't you go take care of what you need to. I'm beat. I wouldn't mind sitting for a sec." He glanced at the TV. "Hey, that's my favorite show," he told Katie. "Mind if I watch?"

Katie shook her head seriously, and Jamie dropped to the floor in the middle of the room. He was alpha male, a warrior, a doer, the kind of man who would always be first in the line of fire and liked it that way. Yet he understood what she needed, that she needed to be there to handle this. And he pulled back so she could have it.

She moved toward the door. "Thanks." And then she left, secure in the knowledge that whatever she found downstairs, whatever else happened, nothing would get through Jamie to get to her sister.

Chapter Ten

Agent Herrera was waiting in her office when Bree walked in on Monday after she'd dropped Katie off at work.

"Heard you had trouble at home. Let me know if there's anything I can do to help," the agent said.

"I appreciate it. Get anything out of Garret about the fake twenty?"

He shrugged. "He got the money at a gas station. It checks out." He scratched his jaw. "But Angel Rivera will be a decent lead, it looks like. He's actually involved, as opposed to coming into connection with the bills unwittingly."

"Did the hospital release him yet?"

"He'll be released in an hour or so. I'm taking him into custody and back to Washington."

"Hope he'll be more forthcoming with you than he was with me."

"He'll talk. If nothing else than for a deal. We got enough on him to put him away for a while. Found a couple of dozen counterfeit bills at his place this morning. Search warrant came through, finally."

"So are the bills from an old print run, just turning up now?"

He shook his head. "New. High-tech paper and ink. We'll definitely be tracking that. I expect we'll find a serious operation."

"Any clues so far? Are bills showing up anyplace else?" She really didn't want any of this connected to her town. The last thing she needed was the CIA descending in large numbers.

"I just got a call about similar bills showing up in Arizona and New York. That's why I'm heading back to the main office. I'll be putting together a task force and widening the investigation."

"Did you find out how Angel Rivera is connected?"

"Not yet. But Rivera works in transportation. He drives a truck for a produce distributor that brings up truckloads of fruit from Mexico. His routes are all over the South and up the Eastern seaboard."

"So the origin of the money could be south of the border?" Honestly, as long as it wasn't her county, she'd be happy.

But the agent shook his head. "Could be,

but unlikely. The technology on these notes is pretty amazing. It's not some handmade printing machine some Mexican farmer threw together from spare parts in his shed."

"There's a paper mill south of the border, not far from here," she told him.

"We'll investigate that to be on the safe side, but this looks like something we usually see from even farther south."

"You mean South America?"

He gave a brief nod. "I'm looking into that. I'll be in touch. I just wanted to come in to thank you for your help. And ask for one more favor."

She waited.

"Angel Rivera has a brother in prison down here. He went in just a few weeks ago on drug charges. He used to work for the same shipping company. Any chance you could look in on him? See if you can push him into admitting to being involved? He's locked up. He'll be more motivated to talk. Maybe in exchange for a reduced sentence. Let me know if you get anything from him."

He shoved his hands into his pockets in a frustrated gesture. "I don't want to wait around, setting up an appointment with the prison when his lawyers can be present and all that. I want to get moving with this. Putting together a task force will take time and paperwork, approvals. I need to be back at the office and set up a serious op. We need to find the source of the money and stop it."

She could certainly understand that. "No problem."

"Even if the younger Rivera doesn't talk, we might be able to use him to soften Angel up a little. Maybe the older brother will give us something in exchange for a promise to make his little brother's life behind bars easier. Prison is a risky place for gangbangers. Not all who go in come out."

She nodded, thinking of the prison hit Jamie was investigating.

"I appreciate the help. We'll keep in touch." Agent Herrera walked to the door of her office, but then turned back before opening it. He watched her for a second before he said, "The other day, I was leaving here when a man was coming in. Is it possible he was Jamie Cassidy?"

Okay, she hadn't expected that question. "You know Jamie?"

"What's he doing here?"

"Consulting for CBP. How do you know him?"

"I was involved in one of his other consulting gigs," he said after a couple of thoughtful seconds.

She had a fair idea what that might have been. "At a time you can't specify, at an undisclosed location, on a mission of indeterminate nature?"

A smile hovered over the agent's lips. "Something like that."

"Was that where he lost his legs?"

The agent shook his head. "He had them there, and put them to good use. It's good to see him back in action. He was the hero of the day."

"Hero, how?"

"I'm sorry. That's confidential information."

"In generalities? I'm assisting his team with something. He's my liaison. I'd like to know what kind of man he is."

He still hesitated for a long second. "Without any specifics… There were bad guys and they land mined a whole village. Jamie's team moved in, at night…." He shook his head. "He was the rear guard. When his teammates were blown up, he rushed in, under heavy gunfire, and dragged them out one by one. He kept going back and getting hit. He didn't stop until he bled out to the point of falling unconscious in the middle of the village. But he got everyone out who could be saved."

She wondered who had saved him. Maybe reinforcements came. She wanted to ask more, but the agent lifted his hand to cut her off.

"This stays between the two of us."

And Bree nodded. "So you don't know how he lost his legs?"

"Not a clue," the agent said. "But I wouldn't be surprised if he threw himself on a grenade." And then he left to go about his business.

She sat behind her desk, thinking for a while about Jamie, about the kind of work he did. Then she set that aside and made a note to figure out what prison the younger Rivera was vacationing at presently. She was going to call his lawyer and see about an appointment to visit later. But first she needed to find Jason Tanner.

Eleanor was dead. Jason couldn't be allowed to hurt anyone else ever again.

She hadn't taken him as seriously as she should have. Her mistake. But she wasn't going to make another with the man. She was going to use every tool at her disposal, call in every favor, track every lead until she found him and put him away.

JAMIE LOOKED THROUGH the database of images he'd been granted temporary access to that morning. Bree had an APB out on Jason Tanner and his red pickup truck, but Jamie had something better: access to military satellites.

No way in hell was he going to let the bastard get within striking distance of Bree again. Jamie needed to track him to his lair.

Jason would be staying somewhere close enough to swing by to see Bree, but not in town where Bree could run into him. Jamie made the whole south part of the county his target. The satellite identified ninety-six images of pickups the color, make and model Tanner was driving, information Eleanor had given the police after the vandalism on the front lawn.

Jason would be holed up in a motel, most likely, so Jamie went after those. He identified seven matching vehicles in motel parking lots and printed the list of addresses.

"I'm off to check on something," he called out to the office in general as he stood from his desk.

Keith and Mo were on office duty, the rest of the team out on the border or following leads.

Mo looked up. "For the deputy?"

Jamie nodded.

"Let us know if we can help," Keith put in, no teasing this time.

They'd all sworn to protect and serve, and the hit on defenseless women didn't sit well with them.

"I appreciate it." He walked out and made his way to his car. He had hours before he had to go back on duty again. Plenty of time to check the addresses on his list.

He first went to the nearest motel he had marked, drove around it, found a red pickup like the one he wanted in the back, but it wasn't Tanner's. This one didn't have a scratch on it.

He was looking for one that had a smashed-in front grill, at least. Those unicorn statues had to have left their mark.

The next address didn't pan out, either. The next after that didn't have a red pickup. Whoever had it might have moved on already.

Jamie made note of that. He would come back if none of the others panned out. For now, he just wanted to do a quick rundown on his list.

He found what he was looking for at the Singing Sombreros Lodge half an hour later. Grill busted, hood dusty, the pickup was hidden in a narrow place between the lodge's two main buildings, parked with its back to the road so the damage in the front wouldn't be easily seen.

Jamie walked around it, tested the door, found it locked. He looked through the window. Nothing incriminating in sight. He could see nothing on the seats beyond fast-food bags and empty beer cans. He left the pickup and walked into the lobby of the main building, flashed his CBP badge.

"Do you have a Jason Tanner registered?"

The clerk, an older man, bald with a Santa Claus beard, scanned the computer screen. He had an antique banjo hanging on the wall behind him. "I'm sorry. I don't see anyone with that name listed."

"Do you know who has the red pickup?"

He frowned. "Some young guy." He looked at his log. "Wait a minute. John Tansey. Here it is. I keep telling him to park that pickup in the lot where it should go. He doesn't listen."

"Room number?"

"Is he in trouble?"

"Yes, he is."

"The guy's having a bad week, I guess. He hit a deer day before yesterday. Banged that nice truck right up. Didn't even save the deer. He's traveling, I suppose. Still, other people would have been happy to take all that venison off his hands. Don't like no waste." He shook his head mournfully. "Room sixty-eight."

"Appreciate it." Jamie looked down the hallway. "Place is full?" He didn't think so, judging by the handful of cars in the lot, but better to double-check. He didn't want anyone getting hurt. It'd be easier for him if the lodge was mostly deserted.

The old man shook his head. "Rodeo crowd cleared out yesterday."

Jamie thanked him again then walked down the hallway toward room sixty-eight. He checked his weapon before he knocked. No response came, but he did hear movement in there, a chair scraping.

"Open up. Customs and Border Protection."

He heard the window open inside. "Put your hands in the air! I'm coming in." Gun in hand, he kicked the door in and caught a flash of a man's back as he jumped out the window.

Jamie dashed across the room and jumped after him. He landed in some landscaping done with stones and cacti, his prosthetics unable to balance on the uneven ground with gravel rolling under his boots. He went down, but was up the next second.

Still, the time wasted added to Jason's lead. He'd already made his way to his pickup and was behind the wheel and driving away, nearly running over Jamie as he ran in front of the car instead of taking a shot at it. He wanted this done without a fatality if he could help it. He and his team were supposed to keep a low profile.

He dove out of the way, rolled and jumped up and ran for his own car. He'd left it unlocked and the keys in the ignition just in case, which came in handy now. He was behind the wheel and after the man within a minute.

The lodge was on the edge of one of the dozens of small towns north of Hullett, the traffic sparse, a straight country road ahead of them. Tanner would have nowhere to go to get out of sight, nowhere to hide. It didn't stop him from running.

The red pickup sped up, sixty-five, seventy, seventy-five, eighty. Jamie kept pace. They were up to ninety-five in another few minutes, Jason running cars that were in his way off the road.

Okay, he was putting other people's lives at risk now. Jamie pulled out his weapon, but didn't aim it at the back of Jason's head.

Even if he wasn't trying to keep a low profile, he only killed if it was an absolute necessity. Tanner wasn't a trained soldier; he wasn't a terrorist. He was a stalker with a mental disability. Catching him would take more work than simply taking him out, but Jamie wanted to give that a go first.

He waited until they came to a stretch of highway that was for the moment deserted save the two of them, then shot out the pickup's back tire.

The vehicle spun almost immediately, went off the road, swerved all around, kicking up a dust cloud as it ran one wheel up a sizable rock that helped to flip it on its side, the tires still spinning as the pickup stopped at last.

Jamie ran his own SUV off the road and circled back, stopped a hundred feet or so from the wreck and got out, keeping his car between him and Jason until he measured up the situation. Jason had to be considered armed and dangerous.

"Come out with your hands in the air!" he called out.

Nothing happened.

"Customs and Border Protection. Come out with your hands in the air, Jason."

But once again, Jason didn't stir. As the dust settled, Jamie moved forward carefully, keeping his weapon aimed at the pickup, watching the cab and the driver's-side door that now pointed skyward, the only possible exit point.

He went around until he could look in the front window. Jason lay flopped over, blood on his forehead. The smell of gasoline filled the air.

The ignition had to be shut off and fast.

Jamie rushed forward, but climbing up the pickup wasn't easy. A long minute passed before he made it up on top. Then he needed both hands to pull the heavy door open, against gravity, seconds passing by during which the both of them could have been sent sky-high by an explosion.

He reached in and turned off the engine first before grabbing for the man. He got hold of an arm and started hauling him up. This was where legs that felt could have come in handy. Finding leverage was difficult like this, on a surface that was uneven, unstable and slippery.

"Come on. Wake up and push, dammit." He gritted his teeth and pulled as hard as he could.

He'd had to decide at one point, after the depression, after he'd fought his demons, that he wasn't going to let anything stop him, and he wouldn't now. Not even when Jason's shirt ripped and Jamie lost balance and fell back off the pickup, the fall rattling his tall frame and knocking the air right out of him.

He got back up and climbed again, this time making sure he got a better hold on the man. He got Jason out halfway, then all the way, lowered him to the ground, slipped down next to him then dragged him a safe distance from the gasoline fumes. On a hot day like this, the sun alone could be enough to ignite something.

"Hey, wake up." He pulled up the guy's eyelid to check his pupils.

And then the man was coming to at last, moaning as Jamie searched him.

No weapon.

"Where is your gun?"

Another moan came in response. Not altogether helpful.

Jamie swore. They were going to need the murder weapon. He wanted a conviction. He wanted to make sure the guy could never come after Bree again. So he ran back to the pickup, climbed back up again, down into the cab and looked for a gun.

Nothing.

Maybe Jason's weapon was still at the hotel. Maybe in his rush to escape he didn't have time to grab it. Or maybe he'd discarded it after the hit, thinking it'd served its purpose.

Did he even know that he'd hit the wrong woman?

Jamie scampered out of the overturned vehicle and went for Jason, who was sitting now and holding his head, still moaning. "Help."

"Stay down." He called Bree. "I got Tanner." He gave his location and a brief explanation. Then he called 911 and asked for paramedics.

GRIEF AND ANGER swirled inside Bree as she watched from behind the two-way mirror as Delancy and another officer questioned Jason Tanner. He'd changed since she'd last seen him. He'd grown taller and filled out, and a five-o'clock shadow covered his face. He fidgeted on his chair, his eyes darting around the room. He was definitely off his meds. When he was taking them, he had an eerie sort of vacant look.

Since she was personally involved in the case, she couldn't go in there. Conflict of interest. At least they had him. And she had Jamie Cassidy to thank for that. She could have kissed him when she'd caught up with him by the side of the road.

The paramedics had already been checking Jason out when she'd arrived. He was scraped up and shaken but hadn't sustained any serious injuries. They'd pronounced him well enough to be taken in.

And now here they all were. Delancy didn't pull her punches as she questioned him.

"I had nothing to do with that," he whined. "My head's hurting."

Jason had admitted to the stalking and photos, even to the vandalism, within minutes. But he denied the shooting. Of course he would. He might have had some mental issues, but he wasn't stupid. He wasn't going to admit to murder.

Bree itched to march in there and confront him. Eleanor was gone, dammit. For what? A decade-old obsession? If she was the crying type, she would have cried over the unfairness of it.

She pushed to her feet and might have barged

in on the interrogation if Lena hadn't opened the door and whispered, "We've got a problem."

Bree hurried out to the hallway. "What is it?"

"Bank alarm just went off. Got a cell-phone call, too. There's someone at the new bank with explosives."

Explosives. Bree stared at her. *Seriously? Now?* "A bank robbery?" She wanted to stay and watch the interrogation unfold.

"Don't know. Sounds like it."

Mercury must have been in retrograde. She glanced around the office, trying to pick who to take with her. There was nobody around. Brian and Delancy were with Jason. The others were out on calls. She couldn't take Lena. Somebody had to stay and man the station.

The insanity never stopped. Welcome to a cop's life. Well, she couldn't complain. She was the one who'd chosen it. And she did love it. On most days.

Chapter Eleven

Her gaze landed on Jamie, who was coming out of the break room with a cup of steaming coffee, watching her.

He'd come in with Jason Tanner. She didn't think he would have waited, but he had, apparently. And he'd heard everything Lena had said. He was walking straight toward them.

"Who's your bomb expert?" he wanted to know.

"Pebble Creek is too small to have its own SWAT team or bomb squad. We call in the pros." Bree nodded to Lena to do just that, then took off running for her car.

If she had to go alone, she had to go alone. Crime didn't stop just because they were at full capacity.

But Jamie was running behind her. "Hang on, I'm coming."

"Not your jurisdiction." She should have stopped him, but she didn't want to spend time arguing. She jumped into her car and took off for the bank, leaving him to do what he wished.

A cruiser was already waiting in front of the bank by the time she reached the building. Mike Mulligan's. Then she saw him, a thirty-year veteran of the force, pushing bystanders back and making sure everyone was safe. Bree parked her own cruiser strategically, so the two would begin forming a barricade to take cover behind.

Jamie, pulling in behind her, did the same. He jumped out and ran toward her. "I can help if you need someone. I know something about explosives."

Of course he did.

"Start evacuating the adjoining buildings," she told Mike, then turned to Jamie. "All right. Fine. Stay back here. I might have to call for you." Then she rushed forward in a low crouch toward the bank's entrance.

She ducked down outside the front door, opened it a crack, held her badge up so whoever was inside could see.

"I'm Bree Tridle, deputy sheriff. I'm here to give you whatever it is you need."

"Too late," came the response from inside—an older male, judging by the tone. He sounded raspy, maybe a smoker.

She didn't recognize the voice, and couldn't

see inside very well through the UV-protection film that covered the glass. All she could make out were shapes.

"How about I come in so we can talk about this?"

"No."

"I can help."

"Can you help me get justice?"

Oh, damn. One of those. Why couldn't it have been over something easy, like money? Justice was a very subjective thing.

"Is killing innocent people justice? Women and children in there?" She could make out two smaller shapes, she thought. Might be kids clinging to their mother.

A moment of silence passed. "Why should I care about them? Nobody cares about me."

"I do. I wouldn't be here if I didn't. Let them go. We'll trade. Me and whatever I can do to help, for them. I'm a cop. I signed up for this. Those people in there didn't. One injustice won't erase another." Whatever it was he thought had been done to him.

More silence stretched between them.

"Those people can't do anything. They can't order anyone to do anything. They have no contacts. No power. I do. I'm the deputy sheriff."

"No trade." His voice shook a little this time. He was getting frustrated.

Okay, no time to waste.

"Then just let me come in. You'll have one more hostage."

And, after an interminable moment, the man said, "Fine." He cleared his throat. "You come in, hands in the air. Leave your gun outside. I see a weapon and we all go to Jesus today."

"Forget her," Jamie called out a foot behind her, scaring the living daylights out of her. How on earth had he snuck up on her? "You don't want a woman in there who'll faint in panic at the first thing that goes wrong. I'm coming in to help. Unarmed."

She shot him a death glare and whispered, "Go away." She could have killed him. They were in the middle of a hostage situation. This was no time for meddling.

"Who the hell are you?" the man inside wanted to know.

"Jamie Cassidy. I work for the United States Government. I can get you things you'll never get from a small-town deputy."

Oh, no, he didn't. Did he just disparage both her sex and her position within the space of a minute? She sent him a Texas death glare.

"Both of you, inside!" the man ordered. "Hands high above your heads."

She turned back to the bank, pulled her weapon from the holster and dropped it on the ground, pushed the door open wide enough to step inside and tried to kick Jamie backward but missed. "We're so going to talk about this," she said under her breath, in a hiss.

He pushed in after her anyway.

In the middle of the main area of the bank, in front of the teller booths, an old man sat in a wheelchair, holding a panicked woman in her twenties in front of him, a handgun pointed at her.

Her eyes wide, her face pale, she looked to Jamie instead of Bree. "Help me!" Her high-pitched voice echoed under the extrahigh, ornately decorated ceiling.

The old man shook her to quiet her. "Untuck your shirts, pull them up and turn around in a slow circle," he ordered in his raspy voice.

Behind him, about a dozen civilians lay face down on the pink marble floor, hands over their heads. Bree sincerely hoped none of them carried concealed weapons and had a mind to start trouble. An amateur shootout was the last thing she needed.

Then again, if someone did have a weapon, they would have probably done something by now.

"Everything is going to be okay," she said to the man with the gun, as much to as the hostages, as she reached for the hem of her shirt.

Jamie did the same, showing off the fact that he'd come in unarmed.

"You should let these people go," Bree said as she tugged her shirt back down. "Whatever complaint you have, I'm sure it has nothing to do with anybody here."

The man watched her for a long moment, exhaustion and desperation in his eyes. He might have thought about what he was going to do here today, but reality was always different. She hoped he was beginning to see at last that this wasn't his best idea.

"Listen. Why don't we just end this now, peacefully, before anybody makes any mistakes? Everybody's scared and tense. But honestly, nobody's hurt." She flashed an encouraging smile. "This is a damn good place to quit."

"You go over there." The man gestured toward the corner with his head, appearing not the least touched by her plea and sound reasoning.

She did as she was asked, and so did Jamie. They slid to the floor next to each other, kept their backs to the wall. The old man in the middle swung the gun to point it at Bree, but he still hung on to the young woman with his other hand, ignoring her whimpering.

Bree stayed as relaxed as she could under

the circumstances and prayed that Jamie would put aside his macho commando instincts for a minute, stay still and not do anything stupid.

Don't escalate. She glanced at him, trying to send him the telepathic message, hoping he got something from the look in her eyes before she turned back to the man in the wheelchair.

"I'm Bree Tridle, as I said, and this is Jamie Cassidy," she added, very nicely. "Would you mind if I asked your name?"

"Antonio Rivera."

She drew a slow breath. Like Angel Rivera? What were the chances it was a coincidence? Very slim.

"You took my son away from me," he yelled at her weakly. "You shot him."

Connection confirmed. Now what? How could she use this to her advantage?

"Only just barely," she said. "Flesh wound. And he shot at me first. He'll be fine." She widened her smile and did her level best to look positive.

"He'll be in jail. His brother is already in jail. What do I have left?"

She had no idea. No wife, she guessed, and scrambled to come up with something.

"Bank's taking the house," the man went on, his face darkening. He adjusted his grip on the gun.

"I'm sorry. Maybe I can work something out with the manager. Do you know Cindy Myers? She sure has a lot of pull at this place. She's very nice, actually. She has two boys, too. Younger than yours. We went to high school together. She'll help you if she can. She's very good that way."

The old man spat on the polished marble floor. "You're just saying that so I let everyone go. I ain't stupid."

"You're holding an entire bank hostage. I know you can figure things out," she said to placate him, while she tried to see what kind of bomb he had.

She spied half a dozen sticks of dynamite. They weren't difficult to come by, unfortunately. Ranchers used them for all kinds of things, including clearing large boulders from their fields.

However, she couldn't see what kind of setup he had under the duct tape that ran around his chest, holding everything in place. She had no idea what he was using for the trigger mechanism, and no idea what to do even if she could spot it, honestly.

She glanced at Jamie, hoping he was catching more than she was, maybe even working on a plan. They sure could have used one of those.

She had no idea whether the SWAT team had arrived yet or when they were coming.

The young woman Antonio held was trembling.

"And what's your name?" Bree asked. Making Antonio realize that she was a real person with a name, somebody's daughter, might help somewhat.

"Melanie."

"Do you have anybody from your family here?" Bree pushed further.

Melanie shook her head and began to cry.

"Shut up," Antonio barked at them.

She couldn't do that, Bree thought, so she took a gamble. "What happened to your legs?"

He might get mad, or he might start talking. Either way, it would gain her time until reinforcements got there.

"What's it to you?" He glared at her, but then he said, "Wire mill."

"I'm sorry. That must have been difficult." She acknowledged him and his troubles. "But you came through it. You'll come through this. Your sons will get out of prison. I'll help you find housing if we can't talk sense into the bank. There's always help available."

"I don't want help," he said darkly. "I just want this to be over with."

The way he said that, the tone of his voice, the bleak look in his eyes, troubled her. Because she knew he meant it. His coming here had never been about getting the bank to change their minds. This was suicide, pure and simple. He just didn't want to go alone.

She drew a slow breath, trying desperately to think of a way out of this, something, anything she could say or do so the standoff didn't end with a bunch of mangled bodies.

"Do you want to speak to Angel? I could probably get him on the phone." She had Agent Herrera's number. "You tell him to cooperate. I'll do anything I can so that he gets a fair deal. Maybe even a reduced sentence."

"Too late." His voice was cold with determination, as bleak as his face.

Melanie sobbed out loud. Some of the hostages squeezed their eyes shut; others stared wide-eyed. A middle-age man was hyperventilating. There was a new kind of tension in the air and they all knew it.

At least there weren't any kids in the bank. She'd been mistaken about that, thank heavens.

But they were out of time.

Jamie shifted next to her.

No, no, no. Her gaze went to him.

He probably had a hidden backup weapon

somewhere on him. He would go for it, then Antonio would set off the bomb, for sure, and they would all die.

EVERYTHING HE WAS pushed him to attack. He'd been trained to charge forward and take down the enemy. He was a warrior. He'd been trained to fight with guns and explosives. His brain and body were weapons.

Jamie shifted again, looking for an angle, a split-second opportunity.

But if he tackled Antonio, the man would set off the bomb. Bree and Jamie were sitting the closest. They'd be toast, for sure. He wasn't as worried about himself, especially if he thought a move like that might save the hostages, but he wasn't willing to risk harm coming to Bree.

"Let me tell you something," he began, and couldn't believe he was talking. It didn't feel even half-right. He was a soldier. He'd been rough and tough pretty much from the beginning and, all right, fine, he might even have been overcompensating a little since he'd been cleared for active duty again.

He didn't have a softer side. For him, to show softness meant to show weakness, which was the dead-last thing he wanted to show, wanted to be.

And yet when Bree's life was at stake…

His usual M.O. of pushing harder wasn't going to work here.

"None of us are here because we want to be," he said. "I'm guessing you'd be doing something a little more fun if you had other choices."

The man glared at him.

Not exactly progress but, hey, they were still alive.

"Between the three of us, we should be able to figure a way out of this," he said, even as part of him was still looking for the man's weak spot, a way to rush him.

SHE SAW HOW he was looking at Antonio Rivera. Bree was pretty sure Jamie would attack, and soon. She wanted to warn him not to, but he wouldn't look at her, and she couldn't say anything out loud for fear of setting off Antonio.

But instead of making his move, Jamie kept talking, his voice low and calm. "I know what you mean. I've been where you are now. Hell of a place."

Other than his words, there was dead silence in the bank, the hostages pretty much knowing this was a Hail Mary effort.

Antonio shot him an angry look. "You haven't. So shut up."

"All right. I'll shut up." He raised his hands

into the air, then pushed to his feet slowly. "But let me show you something."

She held her breath, along with the rest of the hostages.

Antonio moved his gun to point at Jamie's chest.

Slowly, carefully, Jamie reached to his belt, unbuckled it, then unbuttoned and unzipped his pants and let them drop to his ankles.

Antonio stared, along with pretty much everybody.

Jamie's shirt came down to the edge of his boxer shorts, but left the end of his stumps in open view, the skin puckered, white and red scars crisscrossing his skin. For the first time, she got a good look at the straps that held his prosthetics in place.

A couple of women gasped.

She very nearly did, too. Seeing both the living parts and the metal somehow made the sight starker than when she'd rolled up his pant legs before and had seen only the prosthetics. Those were somehow sterile, removed, cold metal. But his scars, the terrible destruction of his living flesh... She swallowed the lump in her throat.

"I didn't want to live," Jamie said in a low voice. "At the field hospital, I begged them to let me die. When they didn't, I promised myself I'd take care of it as soon as I recovered enough and had the strength."

Antonio listened.

"You get to this dark place," Jamie went on. "And it's bad. When you're there, it doesn't seem possible that things will ever get better again. It's like the life outside, the things other people do and see, that's not real. You almost don't even see it."

The hostages watched him silently, barely daring even to breathe.

"Like when you're over there, in the mountains for years on end, people shooting at you, you killing, blood every day. Every day one of your buddies gets blown to pieces. And it seems like that's the only world. Like back here, this was just a dream, the houses and the family and the rain, the banks and the malls and teenagers who go shopping. It's a dream or a fantasy. It doesn't exist. Not to you."

Antonio still pointed the gun at him, but his arm sagged a little.

"Thing is—" Jamie bent slowly and pulled his pants up, buckled his belt "—the other world…it's there. It's real. And the people in it hurt when you leave them."

"Ain't nobody will hurt for me," Antonio said, but his voice wasn't as hard as before.

"Your sons will," Bree put in, talking around

the lump in her throat, thinking about Jamie's seven brothers and the sister he would have left behind if he'd been a weaker man and taken the easy way out. "They cared enough about you to take care of you. They'll hurt."

She drew a slow breath. "And all the families of all the people in here. They are going to hurt and they are going to grieve. People in here have fathers and mothers and kids. They didn't get to say goodbye. Don't make them go through this."

Then everything happened at the same time. Antonio shoved the young woman away from him so he had use of both hands.

Jamie dove for him, but he was too late.

Chapter Twelve

The man blew his own head off a split second before Jamie reached him. As the hostages screamed, all he could do was secure the bomb.

He ignored the blood and gore and the crying and focused on the mechanism. No timer. He looked over the manual control with a flip switch—clearly a home-made job, but with enough of a punch to take out most of the building.

Thing was, as primitively as it was put together, he couldn't guarantee that it wouldn't go off if someone tried to move Antonio. Or if the man's lifeless body slid out of the wheelchair. So he kept working on it as a SWAT team rushed in and spread through the bank, a dozen men dressed in black, holding assault rifles, shouting.

"Everybody down! Everybody down!"

Some of the hostages had leaped to their feet when Antonio had discharged his gun but now flattened themselves to the marble floor once again.

Bree stayed where she was, her hands in the air. "It's okay. Everything's under control. I'm the deputy sheriff. My badge is in my left back pocket."

One of the men checked it for her. "She's okay."

She lowered her hands. "This is Jamie Cassidy. CBP consultant, explosives specialist. He came in with me."

"Status?" the team leader asked.

"One perpetrator. Antonio Rivera. Self-terminated."

"The bomb is still active," Jamie put in as one of the SWAT members rushed over to him, probably their bomb expert. "Simple trigger mechanism. It's a pretty shoddy job. You need to get these people out of here."

The guy checked out the sticks of dynamite and twisted jumble of wires as the rest of his team jumped into action, helping the hostages up and rushing them toward the exit.

"Want to take over?" Jamie offered.

The guy shook his head. "You've got your hand on the wire. Go ahead."

That was pretty much standard operating procedure. The chances of success went up exponentially if the man who started a disarming op was the one who finished it. It wasn't something easily handed over midrace.

He focused on the wires, tracing each to their connections, careful not to set off the trigger. The SWAT guy held Antonio in place, making sure the body wouldn't flop.

"All right. Okay. Almost there."

Then, finally, the last wire was detached.

By that time, there were only three people inside: Bree, Jamie and the man helping him. The SWAT team had cleared the building.

"Well done," the bomb expert said, putting the explosives into the safe box someone had dropped off at some point. "I'll take it from here." He walked away with his precarious charge in his arms.

For the moment, until someone came for the body, Jamie and Bree were alone. They walked away from Antonio, but didn't step outside. Press waited out there, cameras flashing, the news team recording everything. The last thing he needed was his picture on TV. He was an undercover operative.

Bree's eyes were haunted, her face grim as she glanced back at the prone body. "He didn't have to die."

Dead bodies didn't bother Jamie. He was

used to the carnage of battle. But for her… Two violent deaths in the space of days were probably way more than the small town of Pebble Creek was used to seeing. She'd had a pretty tough week.

While he was comfortable with death, he wasn't comfortable in the role of comforter. Yet something inside him pushed him to be just that, for Bree. He filled his lungs and waded into unfamiliar territory.

"We did what we could. It could have been worse. The bomb didn't go off. You kept him distracted for a good long time," he said. He really was impressed with her. "What you did gave the SWAT team a chance to get here."

Her head dipped in a tentative nod. "I thought for sure you were going to rush him, right at the beginning. I thought for sure we'd be toast if you did."

"I thought about it. Then I thought maybe I should try your technique of sweet-talking him. You must be rubbing off on me. I hope there's a cure for that," he teased, hoping it would lift her spirits a little.

"Wouldn't exactly call what you did sweet talk," she said, but gave a tremulous smile.

He reached for her, gratified when she went willingly into his arms. He brushed his lips over hers, relieved beyond words that they were both alive. He had no idea how Mitch Mendoza, his brother-in-law, handled going on joint missions with Megan before she'd taken some time off for the baby. Seeing Bree in danger had been nearly more than Jamie could handle. He would definitely not want to be in a situation like this ever again.

Her fresh, subtle scent, soap mixed with a light perfume, was in his nose, her curves pressed against the hard planes of his body. She was one of those good things he'd given up on at one point in his life. It seemed surreal that here he was, with the woman of his dreams in his arms.

But she was real in every way. And for now, she was with him, lifting her face to his. So he kissed her lightly. Because he really needed to feel her warmth and life and the reality of her being.

Antonio Rivera hadn't been able to let go.

Jamie rested his forehead against hers. He had let go of some things, but not everything, he thought. What if he could let it all go: the past, the pain, the idea that he was a fighting machine and only that?

She made him want to reexamine his assumptions and the way he lived these days. He didn't know if he could, if he should. But he wanted to, for the first time ever.

He dipped back for another taste of her lips.

She tasted so sweet, so right. She was infuriating. He'd nearly had a heart attack when she'd run up to the bank's door to offer herself in exchange for the hostages. Yet, in hindsight, he should have seen it coming. She was no coward. She did whatever she thought had to be done.

She took care of her town; she took care of her sister. He admired her, he realized.

The kiss deepened, yet it still wasn't nearly enough. What would be enough? Would anything ever be enough where Bree was concerned?

He had no idea, he admitted to himself as he pulled away. He had so much darkness around him. In some ways, his past still bound him. She was all light and smiles. He was a surly bastard. He didn't want his darkness to touch her. Temporary slip of willpower or not, he simply wasn't the right guy for her.

He would have told her that, but people were filing in through the door. Some of the SWAT team were coming back to finish their business.

A BOMB IN a bank, with a fatality added, required enough paperwork to make her head spin. She would have more follow-up work the next day, but she had to set that aside and go get Katie, so Bree powered off her computer and locked up her office.

Jason Tanner was in holding, his parents notified. They retained a lawyer for him. He'd confessed to the photos and the unicorn massacre, but he would not budge on the shooting. Maybe tomorrow, Bree thought. Tomorrow was another day.

The station was buzzing; some of the bank hostages were still there, giving statements, something Lena and Mike were more than capable of handling.

"Tell Katie I said hi," Lena called over as Bree told them she was leaving for the day.

The events at the bank crowded into her head as she drove, as she went over what she could have done to achieve a better ending to the standoff. She was the one who'd caught Angel Rivera. Angel had made bad choices. So had Antonio, in the end. Could she have done anything differently?

She was deputy sheriff, but she couldn't say she was happy when someone went to jail or died, even if they were criminals. First and foremost, she was a peace officer. She wanted peace for her people. Which was why she made sure crime prevention was a very real program in the county, not just a political hobbyhorse to be dragged out at sheriff elections.

She looked in the mirror to make sure she looked okay before she picked up Katie. She drew a deep breath and forced a smile on her face. *No bringing the job home.* The only fast and hard rule she never broke.

She pulled over in front of the big yellow building where her sister worked, and Katie jumped into the car and started talking about her day immediately. Katie lived in the here and now, always. It was an amazing way to live, one that Bree sometimes envied. No worries, no regrets, no self-blame.

"Mrs. Springer brought cupcakes today," she was saying. "They were chocolate with chocolate frosting. They had chocolate sprinkles."

Bree pulled into traffic. "You can never have too much chocolate."

"That's what she said. Except when you're a dog, because chocolate kills dogs. Then even a little is too much."

"Very true."

"We don't have a dog."

"No, we don't. We have unicorns."

"Scott said once they had a burglar and their dog chased it away."

Bree glanced at Katie then back at the road. They'd had some scary vandalism, then a fatal shooting at the house within the space of a week. Just because Katie lived in the now didn't mean she didn't have logic. She did, and plenty of it. And maybe logic said that if bad things could happen at their house as they had, they could happen again.

"You know the bad guy we talked about?"

Katie nodded.

"We caught him today. Jamie did, this morning. The bad guy is going to jail. All locked up."

"And can't get out."

"That's right."

"Scott was in a car accident once," Katie said. It was a non sequitur, and they talked about that next.

She saw Jamie's SUV in front of her house as soon as she turned onto her street. He'd gone into work after they parted at the bank. He only had half a shift, as Mo had to do something with his stepson and they'd traded time.

His seat was tilted back, she saw as she came closer. He seemed to be asleep. Good. He deserved some rest.

Katie got out and went straight to the front door with the keys. She loved locking and unlocking things, and any kind of lock mechanism. She could play with a combination lock for hours when she'd been younger.

She had a whole collection she'd accumulated over the years. Some she'd picked up with their mother on garage-sale outings—their standing Saturday morning mother-daughter date that had since been replaced by hanging out with Sharon. Many other locks since, even antique ones, had been given as gifts by friends—several by Eleanor. Katie could remember the combination to every single one of them.

Bree walked over to Jamie's car. He had all the windows rolled down, probably to catch a breeze.

His eyes were open by the time she reached him. "Hey."

Her gaze caught on a bundle of yellow police tape on his backseat. He'd gathered that up from around her property. So Katie wouldn't have to see it and remember.

Her heart turned over in her chest. "Hey."

"Thought I'd stop by to make sure everything was okay."

"Jason's in jail. Thanks to you. I think we're done with trouble for a while. Hopefully."

He nodded, looking tired and rumpled with bristles covering his cheeks; he was so incredibly sexy, he took her breath away.

"What are you going to do about that busted living room window?" he wanted to know. "It doesn't look too safe the way it is."

She glanced at the empty frame. The contractor who worked with the police station, people who cleaned up crime scenes, had taken away the broken glass when they'd come to clean up the blood inside. She'd recommended them to families of victims many times in the past. They did excellent work. But they didn't do repairs.

"I called it in. Should be fixed tomorrow. It's a standard-size window, so at least I didn't have to do special order." That would have taken forever.

"How about I hang out on your couch tonight?"

He was asking and not telling her. Definite progress from Jamie Cassidy.

"It's not exactly a high-crime area. And I'm well-armed. I'm kind of the deputy sheriff."

The corner of his mouth lifted a little. "For my peace of mind, then."

Because he cared?

There went that funny feeling around her heart again.

"You're just here for the triple-winner breakfast," she joked. "Nobody can resist my salsa egg scramble."

His lips tilted into an almost smile. "Maybe." And then he got out, unfolding his long frame, and followed her in.

Katie was already going through her predinner routine.

"Jamie is having dinner with us." Bree took off her gun harness and hung it in its place, out of reach, although she didn't have to worry about Katie. Her sister was excellent with remembering and following rules to a T.

"Hi, Katie."

"Hi, Jamie." She glanced through the hole in the window at her unicorns, and seemed to have no problem with Jamie being there. She skipped to the kitchen cabinet and grabbed another plate.

Bree went upstairs and changed into a pair of jeans and a tank top, then padded back down to start dinner. Fried chicken steak, an old Texas staple, was one of Katie's favorites.

"What can I do to help?"

She stopped for a moment to look at him. "When was the last time you slept?" He worked long hours for his team, then he was helping her in between.

"I'm good."

"I have a well-oiled dinner routine with Katie. How about you lie down on the couch for a minute?"

He raised an eyebrow. "So because I'm a man, you assume I'd be no good in the kitchen and you're telling me to stay out of the way? Very sexist."

"Deal with it." But she was smiling as she shook her head. "You'll get to do manly things later," she said, without really thinking about how that sounded until his face livened up.

"Not what I meant." She tried to backpedal, laughing.

He looked skeptical, one dark eyebrow rising slowly. "What did you mean, exactly?"

"Like chopping wood out back." Or something like that.

He didn't look convinced.

So she turned to the stove while he walked off to take a predinner nap.

She didn't think anyone could sleep through the pots banging and Katie's chatter, but he did. He must have been truly exhausted. But he rolled right to his feet when she finally finished the gravy and called him to dinner.

She could barely concentrate on the food. She was too distracted by the man at her table. He had a presence that filled up her kitchen.

But while he filled Bree with awareness that tingled across her skin, Katie was acting as if he was a member of the family and his eating dinner with them happened every day. For some reason, maybe because of the great unicorn rescue, she had accepted him fully and unconditionally.

"Excellent dinner. I appreciate the invitation," he said over his plate. And ate like he meant every word.

He probably didn't get many home-cooked meals, she supposed, liking that he appreciated her cooking.

"He's making the happy face," Katie put in.

"Yes, he is." Bree put a happy face of her own into play.

Her awareness passed after a while, and she began enjoying their dinner together. There was such a warm, homey feeling, such a normalcy to them sharing a meal. Maybe because of his nap, maybe because of the meal, the harsh lines on Jamie's face relaxed for once and stayed that way.

She liked this. She liked it a lot.

Not smart. She sighed. *Heartbreak ahead.* Her head sounded the warning.

Too late. She was enough of a realist to know

that there was nothing she could do to stop herself from falling for him.

WHAT THE HELL was he doing here? Jamie thought as he lay on the couch in Bree's living room in the middle of the night, staring at the ceiling.

She didn't need him. She was a good cop. She could take care of herself. Jason Tanner was in jail. And as she'd said, she lived in a pretty good neighborhood.

He hadn't been lying when he'd asked to stay for his own piece of mind. Bree mattered. And so did Katie. She was a sweet kid. Quick, too. She'd put together a puzzle of Klimt's *The Kiss* before he finished a small corner.

Of course, the painting the puzzle created put kissing into his mind. And Bree. And he hadn't been able to clear those images out of his head since. His emotions and thoughts were in a jumble. He didn't like that. He was used to always having a clear battle plan.

Except, this was no battle.

So why was he fighting his own feelings?

He rolled to his feet. He hadn't taken his prosthetics off. While it was unlikely that anyone would break in, he wanted to be ready if there was trouble.

He walked across the room then stopped, thought some more about what he was doing. He was very likely making a mistake. He walked up the stairs, anyway.

He knocked as quietly as he could, prepared to go back down if there was no answer.

"Come in."

He pushed the door in slowly, not entirely sure he should.

She sat up in bed, the worn police academy T-shirt she wore as a nightgown covering most of her, except for her amazing legs. He could have stood there staring at her forever.

She swung her feet to the ground as if to stand up, but then she didn't.

He moved to her without words and sank to his knees in front of her, pulled her closer, her legs on either side of him as he rested his forehead against her collarbone.

"I couldn't sleep," he said against her T-shirt, breathing in her soapy scent. He liked the way she smelled, the way she felt, the way she fit against him.

Her head lowered, her lips coming to rest in his hair. "Me, neither."

He looked up into her face, which was illuminated by the moonlight. Time for the naked truth. "I want you."

For a nerve-racking moment, she didn't say anything, but then she smiled.

Oh, man. Maybe it would have been better if she sent him away. "I don't know how it's going to work."

Her smile turned into a wicked grin. "A virgin? Don't worry. I'll be gentle."

And he couldn't help but smile back. She could make him smile like nobody else. It was a miracle. He really had been a grouchy bastard over the past couple of years.

To be honest, he almost did feel like a virgin. She was like no other. He didn't want to mess this up. He didn't want to repulse her.

"Step one would be to lock the door," she advised him.

And he got up to do that. When he came back to her, he sat next to her on the bed.

"Okay, so the first part is called foreplay." She shifted onto his lap. "Tell me if I'm going too fast and you don't understand something. We'll go back and repeat whatever step you're having trouble with."

"You're a good instructor," he said as his arms went around her.

"I train rookies at the station all the time."

He threw her a questioning look.

She smothered a laugh. "Not in this!"

"I hope not," he said with a sudden shot of jealousy, as he pulled her head down to his for a kiss.

She was in his arms, her lips pressed against his, her arms wound around his shoulders. His entire body was alive and hardening with desire within seconds.

He deepened the kiss and took what he needed. She didn't protest. When she dug her fingers into the short hair at his nape, desire rippled down his spine.

He wanted her. She was the only woman he'd wanted in a very long time. This was not something spur of the moment; this was not trivial. The two of them in this room meant something, something he wasn't sure he was ready for.

But he couldn't walk away from her.

He shifted them until they were lying side by side on the bed.

Okay, that was smoother, so far, than he'd expected. He was up on one elbow next to her, their lips still connected. He had a free hand. He was a soldier, trained to take advantage of every tactical advantage.

"I don't know what you're doing. Here with me. You're perfect. I'm…" He was going to say messed up, but she cut him off.

"Stubborn?"

"No way."

"Surly?"

"When warranted."

Then he forgot what they were talking about as he tugged up her T-shirt and put his hand, fingers stretched out, on her flat stomach. Her skin was warm and smooth and begged to be explored. He moved his fingers upward.

She gave a soft groan and lifted her chest.

He wanted to be inside her so badly it hurt.

His hand cupped her breast; there was no bra, just warm skin and a pebbled nipple that he was ready to taste. He pulled up the soft material and lowered his lips to the tight bud.

Her hands kneaded his shoulders, her head tilted back.

"Take it back. I'm not perfect," she said in a whisper.

"What?" His mind was in a haze. He lifted his head.

She shifted to look at him. "I'm not perfect."

"A whole state begs to differ. You were Miss Texas. Don't you miss the beauty-queen days?"

She looked away.

"What is it?"

"My mom wanted that." She turned back to him. "She wanted me to be extraperfect, maybe because Katie wasn't.... I didn't really like the beauty-pageant thing."

He watched her, the emotions crossing her face.

"When my parents died in the fire, I was devastated. Then a few days later, when we were picking through the ashes, I came across some of my pageant wardrobe, all charred. And I thought, with Mom gone, I'd never have to go up on stage again. And I had never before felt such relief in my life." Her voice broke.

He held her closer. "And you felt guilty."

"I wasn't relieved that my mother was dead."

He kissed her. "You were relieved that you didn't have to live a life you never chose. It's not like you shirk responsibility. You take care of Katie."

"That's different. I want to. I love being with her."

He kissed her again, amazed that she would share this with him, that she trusted him enough to open up. This was about more than sex, a warning voice said in his head. For the both of them.

He ignored the voice. His body wanted what it wanted. He went back to kissing her soft skin.

His mouth made the trip back to hers, lingering on her delicious neck in between, then back down to the other nipple. He wanted to keep kissing her for hours, but the urgency building in his body pushed him to take things to the next level.

He rolled her under him, pulled up her knees, one then the other on either side of him, pressed his hardness against her soft core and groaned with the sharp pleasure of the contact. He rocked into her, kissed her over and over, and that was enough for a few more minutes. Then it wasn't.

He shifted them again and pulled her shirt over her head, while she did the same with his, their arms tangling. She was down to her skimpy underwear, her soft skin glowing in the moonlight, bared for him.

She reached for his belt buckle. Because there was no hesitation in her, he didn't feel any, either. He helped her.

She tugged down his pants. He reached for his prosthetic leg on one side. She watched what he did and helped him on the other side, her fingers frenetic and impatient.

Because she wanted him.

With everything he was and he wasn't.

Then the metal was gone, then her underwear, then his. She whisked out a foil wrap-

per from her nightstand and helped him with
that, too.

He loved the feel of her hands on him.

He moved to cover her amazing body with
his. Then his erection was poised at her opening for a second before he sank into her moist,
tight heat. His mind exploded first, then his
heart.

The distance, the walls he'd built, the darkness he'd carried, they all fell away.

There was only Bree.

Chapter Thirteen

Bree woke alone, and after a second, she could vaguely remember Jamie kissing her goodbye before he went into work at dawn.

Her body felt like…cotton candy—a big fluff of happiness. She couldn't stop grinning. Even the toothpaste ran down her chin while she brushed her teeth.

She dropped Katie off at work, went into the office and did some more paperwork regarding the incident at the bank the day before. She wanted to talk to Jason Tanner, still in lockup, but thought better of it. She didn't want to mess up this case. She didn't want him to get off on a technicality.

He needed to be held responsible for what he'd done, be locked up and get help for his mental problems. As he was now, he was a danger to society.

Instead of going back to his holding cell with her questions, she called around to see when she could go over to the prison to talk to Angel Rivera's younger brother. She wasn't looking forward to having to tell him about his father's death at the bank. Angel would have to be told, too, so she sent off a quick email to Agent Herrera about that.

Since she couldn't talk to the younger Rivera without his lawyer present, she tracked that information down first.

"You gotta be kidding me," she murmured as she took in the screen. Steven Swenson. Or Slimeball Swenson, as he was known in law-enforcement circles.

He had very little regard for the law, and none whatsoever for the police. He'd sued probably every police department in the county at one point or another. Everything the cops did was an "overreach of power" in his book, and he was happy to cause as much trouble as humanly possible.

He was famous for his utter lack of cooperation. She so did not look forward to having to talk to him. She made the call, anyway. When he didn't pick up, she was almost relieved, even if she knew she'd have to try again. She left him a message.

She went through some more paperwork, handled some walk-ins then braced herself and called Swenson again. Still nothing. The guy didn't call her back, either. He wouldn't. The word "helpful" was completely missing from his dictionary.

The next time her phone rang, it was Jamie on the other end.

"Hi. Sorry I left so early."

Her heart leaped at the sound of his voice, images from the night before flashing across her brain. Parts that had no business tingling when she was on duty came awake. "You had work."

"I just don't want you to think I was doing the 'guy runs away in the morning' thing. I wanted to stay."

The quiet admission made her heart swell. "I can't see you running away from anything. You're not the type."

"Neither are you."

"No," she agreed.

He hesitated for a moment. "So what are we going to do about this?"

"We figure it out as we go," she said tentatively, expecting him to come up with ten reasons why a relationship between them couldn't work. Heck, she could have come up with twenty on her own.

But instead, he said, "Okay." Then he said,

"Lunch? I can probably get away for half an hour. I'm on office duty today."

"I'm going to take a working lunch. I need to see a guy's lawyer."

"Have fun."

"Not with this one. It's Slimeball Swenson." She was going to drive by and see if she could catch him in person.

"Hostages are suing already?"

"No. Nothing to do with the bank. It's about the counterfeiting case. I'm tying up a loose end for the CIA agent in charge."

"I'll see you tonight?"

Her heart leaped again. "Like you ever asked permission before for barging into my life without notice?"

He chuckled on the other end.

She'd wondered once what it would take to see him smile. And now that she'd seen him smile… She was rapidly falling for him.

Don't get ahead of yourself. Don't get your heart broken. It was one night. Neither of them wanted anything permanent. They both had their lives set up in a way that worked for them.

"I'll see you tonight, then," he said. "Especially if you have leftover chicken steaks."

And even if it was something temporary,

whatever they had between them, she felt a thrill at the prospect of spending another night with him. "You only like me for my cooking."

"I pretty much like everything about you, Bree."

Her heart gave a hard thud. "Now you're just angling for dessert." She made a joke of it, even though she was ridiculously pleased.

After they hung up, she called Swenson again. Maybe he was with a client and that was why he wasn't answering. She left him another message, telling him she was coming over.

But before she could get away, a couple of teenagers were brought in: a drug bust. She handled that; one set of parents was belligerent, blaming everyone but their offspring, the other apologetic.

A full hour passed before she could drive off to see Swenson over in Hullett, her mind wandering to how incredibly good Jamie and she had been together and what she was going to do about that. A complicated question, so she drove the back roads, giving herself a few extra minutes to think.

She was so preoccupied that she was at the reservoir by the time she noticed that a dark van was following her. All the windows were tinted, so she couldn't make out the faces in the front, only two menacing dark shapes.

They were the only two vehicles on the abandoned road. She sped up. So did the van. It kept gathering speed, closing the distance between them.

"JUST WANTED TO see how you were doing," Jamie told his sister, Megan, over the phone as he sat behind his desk at the office. "How is baby Bella?"

"As grouchy as you are. She's teething." His sister made some nonsensical baby noises on the other end.

You couldn't tell now that she was a tough undercover operative. In fact, she'd met her husband on a South American op where they'd nearly killed each other before they'd fallen in love.

"Oh," she said. "You should see her. You wouldn't believe how fast she's growing. She's a little champion at breastfeeding. Aren't you, my little moochy-woochy?" She cooed.

He winced.

He'd only seen the baby once, in the middle of a screaming fest. He had no idea why people had babies. Forget mortal combat, babies were scarier.

"Are you calling to volunteer to babysit?" his sister wanted to know.

Right. Maybe in an alternate universe. "Sorry, too busy saving civilization as we know it."

"Sure, use that old excuse," Megan said in a droll tone, but then she laughed. "How are you? Is working stateside strange? How are the guys? God, they're hot. Don't tell Mitch I said that. How is the job?"

"Good."

She waited.

"Everything's okay."

"Well, no sense singing a whole ode about it. You know how I hate when you talk my ear off. Sheesh, what are we, like girlfriends?"

"Very funny."

"I'm known for my sense of humor. And loved for it." She cooed to the baby again before returning to him. "So you're calling to tell me what, exactly?"

"Just to see how you all are doing."

A moment of silence passed. "Is there a woman?"

"What? On earth? Over three billion and counting. Some of them are pretty annoying."

"I know for sure you're not talking about me." She paused for a second. "I think there's a woman. You're softening. Is she the type to babysit?"

Probably. "There's no woman."

"Well, she's obviously good for you," Megan went on, ignoring his declaration. "When do we get to meet her?"

Family. A synonym for people who stick their noses into your business and enjoy it. "Oh, look. I better go. Terrorists are attacking. They're coming out from all over the jungle—"

"Yeah, whatever. You're calling from your office phone. I can see the number on my display and—" The baby cried in the background. "All right. But we'll talk about this mystery woman later. Take care of yourself. We all love you, Jamie."

His throat closed up suddenly. "I love you, sis. Give a kiss to my favorite niece for me."

He hung up and thought about his family, the rest of them. He really should be in touch more often. He thought about the baby. He should send her a gift. He would have to ask Bree what would be appropriate. She would know. She was good with family. She was good with pretty much everything. He would ask her for some advice tonight.

With that resolution made, he turned back

to his computer, to the task he'd interrupted to make the spur-of-the-moment call.

He so wasn't the spur-of-the-moment, check-on-family kind of guy. Maybe Megan was right and he *was* softening. Great. Just what he didn't need.

He looked through the secondary list from the prison where Jimenez had been recently incarcerated, scanned pages the warden's office had emailed him and checked the list of attorneys visiting clients on the day the kill order had been passed to Jimenez. A name jumped out at him: Steven Swenson. Might be Slimeball Swenson, the attorney Bree had just mentioned on the phone.

He tapped his finger on his desk as he stared at the screen, bad premonitions sneaking up on him.

So the same lawyer was representing the guy she was investigating for counterfeit money, and the guy Jamie was investigating for doing a hit for the Coyote. If Slimeball Swenson was the one who'd carried the hit order to Jimenez from the Coyote, then he was one of the Coyote's men, too. From what they knew about him, the Coyote worked with some of the most ruthless killers in the business.

And Bree was on her way to Swenson.

He dialed her number, a thousand fears cutting through him while he waited for her to pick up.

"Jamie!"

The sickening crunch of metal that followed the single word had him on his feet. "Where are you?"

"On the old mining road by the reservoir. There's a van behind me."

"Steven Swenson," he called to Shep as he ran for the door. "Local attorney. Find him. He's the Coyote's man. Send someone to pick him up." Then he was through the door, clutching the cell phone to his ear. "Are you okay?" he asked Bree.

"They're trying to push me into the water. I don't think—"

Another sickening crunch came.

"Bree?" He ran for his car and shot out of the parking lot, heading for her.

She didn't respond. Maybe she'd dropped the phone. She probably needed both hands on the steering wheel.

The way he was driving, so did he, so he switched to Bluetooth and tossed the phone onto the passenger seat. He could hear her yelling on the other end, car tires squealing.

His heart pounded.

"I'm coming," he said, in case she could somehow hear him. "Hang in there. I'm on my way."

Thank God the back roads were clear. He made the half-hour drive in fifteen minutes, the longest fifteen minutes of his life. He got there just in time to see Bree's cruiser tumble into the dark water of the reservoir, pushed by the van behind her.

He rolled down his window and shot at the van with his left hand. He had no hope of hitting anyone, but if he could scare them off, it would be enough.

He kept shooting, emptying his clip, slammed a second one into place and shattered the van's back window at last. He could see two men in the front, hunched over the dashboard to avoid his bullets. One of them shot back, but then they finally decided they wanted to stay alive and the van sped away.

Then he was at the water's edge, jumping from his car, kicking off his pants, taking off the metal that would have dragged him down, and dove in, sinking.

He'd learned how to swim without legs, but not well enough. He'd focused too much on the other aspects of his physical therapy, like regaining his balance on dry land and how to adjust his hand-to-hand combat skills so his moves would still work with the new reality of his body.

Now he wished he'd spent more time in the pool.

He used his arms to maneuver himself forward in the murky water toward the spot where he'd seen Bree's cruiser sink. If all he could do was help her out of her car and somehow push her up, even if he stayed on the bottom, he'd be happy.

BREE FREED HERSELF from the car just to get tangled in a giant ball of wire someone had dumped into the reservoir. Probably illegal dumping from the wire mill. She was so going to issue a ticket for that. If she lived.

She struggled to swim, dragging the heavy ball of metal behind her. She bumped up to the surface for one quick gulp of air before the weight dragged her back down.

She doubled her efforts and made it up to the air again. But with the tangle of metal hanging from her left foot, she couldn't stay afloat. She went back down again.

She could go up a few times, she realized, but when she got tired, the wire would permanently anchor her to the bottom. She gritted her teeth and went down instead of up this time, trying to untangle herself from her anchor.

The inch-wide wire was slimy with rust and algae. Her fingers kept slipping without being able to find a good grip.

When her lungs began to burn, she abandoned her efforts and swam up for another gulp of air, dragging the weight with her. She could only stay up for seconds before the wire pulled her down again. Her arms and legs were tiring.

How many times could she do this? One more time? Twice? Certainly no more than that.

Desperation squeezed her chest.

The wire cut into her ankle, into her fingers as she tore at it. This time, when she went up for air, she had to struggle harder to make it.

Chances were she was going to die here, she thought on her way down again. There were only two things she regretted. That she would leave Katie alone, and that she hadn't told Jamie Cassidy that she cared about him.

But even as she thought about Jamie, he appeared in the murky water next to her. He scared her half to death for a split second before she recognized him and sharp relief washed through her.

He helped her with the wire, shoved her up even as he sank a little. She got hold of his arm, then kicked away toward the surface.

Then she could breathe again, and he was

right there, the two of them dragging, pushing each other toward shore like some weird, desperate tag team. When they finally made it out, they could do little more than lie in the mud on their backs and gasp for air.

"I didn't get them." He coughed up water. "I let them get away."

Her lungs burned. She was ridiculously grateful just to be alive. "I'm so glad you showed up. I was running out of steam fast. You saved my life."

"It's not enough. I want to know who's after you, dammit. I should have caught those men."

She brushed the wet hair out of her face. "Oh, well... As long as you're playing God, maybe you can do something about the drought. I'm sure a lot of Texas farmers would be grateful."

He turned his head from her.

A moment passed before she realized he was looking at his prosthetics, a few hundred feet away. He got up and maneuvered himself that way, supporting his weight on his hands.

Her gaze caught on the way his wet shirt stuck to his back and upper arms, outlining his muscles. Those were the arms that had saved her. He had an incredible body. She didn't think she could ever get tired of looking at him.

He strapped his legs on then pulled up his pants.

"You know, we do have a public-indecency ordinance in place. You seem to have a habit of going pantless in public," she remarked as she stood and squeezed water out of her hair and clothes.

He glanced back as he got to his feet. "You going to arrest me for that?"

She sighed. "I kind of like it. Does that make me shallow?"

Surprise crossed his face, then a half smile formed. "You're not what I expected."

"Is that good or bad?" she asked as she caught up with him.

But instead of answering her question, he said. "Don't drown again. It makes me feel..." He shrugged.

She watched him for the rest, but he didn't finish.

"Were you scared for me? Is this a mucho-macho thing? Not admitting to being scared? For the record, I was terrified."

He reached for her, caught her arm and pulled her close. He dipped his head to hers and brushed his mouth over her lips. "I was scared for you. I don't think I've ever been this scared."

"I'm a tough Texas deputy."

He gave a rare full smile at that. "I know. And the stupid thing is…" He glanced down then back up to hold her gaze. "I feel like I don't want to let you out of my sight. Ever."

Oh. Warmth spread through her chest. It quickly turned to full-on heat when he kissed her.

They were wet and dirty from lying in the mud. There was a van with armed men out there somewhere who wanted her dead. Since she figured the chances of catching up with them at this stage were ridiculously slim, she gave herself over to the kiss.

Live in the moment. She'd learned that from her sister.

And after a few seconds, she could barely remember where they were or how they'd gotten here. The thing about Jamie was he could transport her in an instant to some place where she could barely remember reality. He was a seriously good kisser. He kissed her as if she was the most important thing in the universe to him, the only thing.

That kind of stuff could go to a woman's head.

They fit together perfectly. They moved in unison, each knowing what the other wanted without a word having to be said. She'd never felt like this with anyone before.

"You're not what I expected, either," she told him when they finally pulled away.

He looked her over. "I'll take you home. You need to change."

"Will I see you tonight?"

He nodded.

"I'll have dinner ready." God, they sounded like an old married couple. It pleased her to no end.

But he didn't show up that evening. He was called in to deal with some smugglers on the border, so she spent the night alone, having to be content with only dreaming about him.

Chapter Fourteen

The following morning, Jamie sat in his SUV outside Steven Swenson's house, Bree next to him. Swenson worked out of his converted garage, which served as his home office. He was a one-man law firm. Maybe nobody wanted to work with him. According to Bree, he was pretty much a jerk.

Jamie's team, as well as Bree's, had searched the house and office the day before, but the man had been gone.

Taped to Jamie's dashboard were printouts of half a dozen versions of what he might look like if he came back wearing a disguise. With a beard, with a bald head and so on. Bree's idea. She had some computer program at the station.

Swenson had small, close eyes, a crooked nose and a cruel mouth topped with a mustache that was yellow from smoking. Tall and skinny with a slightly bent back, he even looked like a weasel.

"He'll be back," she was saying, watching the house. "It doesn't look like he took much. He left in a hurry."

They hadn't found anything incriminating either in the house or in the office. Then again, Swenson had passed the bar exam, presumably, at one point. He was probably smart enough not to keep a log of his illegal business with the Coyote.

Because life was never easy.

"You called to let him know that you were coming over," Jamie said. "He probably thought you were onto some of his dirty dealings. He panicked, ordered a hit then took off until the dust settles."

"I'm betting he's connected to the counterfeit money."

"And to the Coyote, too. Should have figured those two were linked." Why not? The Coyote ran human smuggling, guns and drugs. It made sense that he would have a hand in everything that was illegal and big business. He controlled a large area and a veritable army of criminals.

Not for long; Jamie's team always got their men.

"What if Swenson doesn't come back?" Bree asked.

The bastard had tried to have Bree killed, Jamie thought as he looked at her. He could never look at her without being a little daz-zled. "Then I'm going to track him to the ends of the earth."

She shook her head at him. "You know, from anyone else that would sound like fake action-movie dialogue, but when you say it, I know you actually mean it."

He smiled at her. She got him. He liked that. He liked way too many things about her.

"He didn't go south," she said as she glanced at the abandoned house once again. "Border agents are watching for him. I put out an APB yesterday. He could be holed up somewhere else."

"He owns no other properties beyond this place. He has no siblings. Mother and father dead. Never been married." Jamie had run the guy through the system as soon as he'd gotten back to the office the day before.

"He could be with friends," she said, then thought for a second before continuing. "Who does he trust?"

"A guy like that? Probably nobody. I wouldn't if I was in his place." If he was caught, the law was the least of his problems. He knew very well that the Coyote could reach people in prison, have them killed.

"He's lying low somewhere. We have a state-wide APB out on him and his car. Every cop in Texas is looking for him. I'm betting he knows that."

Jamie drummed his fingers on the steering wheel as he ran a couple of possibilities through his brain. "He represents criminals. Most of them are in prison. Which one of his clients has a place that stands empty?"

He pulled out his phone and called that in, talked to Mo on the other end. Mo and Keith were in the office, with access to information a regular sheriff's office could only dream of.

"I'll run some queries," Mo said. "I'll call you back when I have something."

"Thanks." Jamie put the phone down, trying to think what else they could be doing.

Bree shifted in her seat, turning to him. "When your top-secret mission is done here, will you all be leaving?"

"The office has been made permanent. The border needs to be monitored. CBP is set up for illegal immigration. Terror threats are a whole diffcrent level, and the problem is not going to go away in the foreseeable future. It needs different people with different training."

"I'm glad," she said. "That you and your team are here. I wasn't at the beginning when I first found out about it."

They talked a little more about that, how times were changing. They kept watching the house, seeing no suspicious movement. Half an hour passed before Mo called back.

"I have an address for you. I found a couple of things, but I think our best chance is a remote farmhouse. One of Swenson's clients inherited it from his parents recently. The guy's sitting in federal prison. Swenson is trying to sell the place for him to cover legal expenses for an appeal."

"Thanks. We're heading over. I'll call in to let you know what we find when we get to the place." Jamie punched the address into the GPS and took off.

"You need backup?"

"Let's wait and see if he's even there. And I've got Bree."

"Thanks," she said as he hung up.

"For what?"

"For treating me as an equal partner."

He wasn't sure what to say as he flew down the road, heading for the highway.

"This way." She pointed in a different direction. "I know a dirt-road shortcut."

Which was why he looked at her as a partner. She knew what she was doing. Still, as much as he trusted and admired her skills, he did feel a sense of protectiveness at the thought of her going into danger.

Maybe he should have asked for that backup.

"What if he's not alone? What if the men who pushed you off the road are with him?"

"I really hope so," she said as she checked her weapon, flashing the first scary smile he'd seen on her.

In another five minutes he reached the dirt road and turned onto it. His SUV bounced over the gravel. In a little while, they could see the abandoned farmhouse in the distance, surrounded by outbuildings. A red-and-blue For Sale sign greeted them from one of the front windows.

"Swenson's last stand," Bree said.

He scanned the ranch. "No cars."

"He'd be smart enough to pull his car into the barn. He knows we're looking for him. How close do we pull up?"

He could see tire tracks in the gravel driveway in front of them. Somebody had definitely been out this way lately. Of course, it could be anybody, even people who were looking to buy the place.

"We'll pull up all the way. I don't think he'd start shooting right away. He'll hope we think the place is abandoned and drive away. He's a lawyer, not a sharpshooter. He hires out his dirty business. He'll try to avoid a shootout with law enforcement if he can. He knows the odds are not on his side."

"So what's the plan?"

"We pull up, keeping in the cover of the car as we get out. If there's no attack, we'll walk around the outbuildings first." He slowed the car as they reached the end of the driveway, the gravel crunching under the tires.

"We'll make our way to the shed," she said. "That's closest to the end of the house. He might only have a small bathroom window there, or none. I'll stay somewhere visible from the front windows to distract him. You sneak up to the side."

"Exactly." Man, it was easy to work with her. She had a quick mind.

"How do I know when to come after you?"

You don't. You stay where it's safe, he wanted to tell her, but he knew her well enough to know that she wouldn't accept that. And he did trust her to handle herself.

"If things go well, if he's in there, I'll bring him out through the front door. If things go badly, you'll hear the shots." They were both wearing Kevlar vests.

"All right. Let's get him."

He stopped the car and pulled his weapon out, waited. Nobody shot at them. So far, so good. He opened his door. No movement in the house. He stepped to the ground but stayed behind the open door for a second as he scanned his surroundings. Still nothing. Then he stepped to the side and closed the car door.

He was out in the open.

If Swenson was in there and he was going to do something stupid, this was the time to do it. But nothing happened. Jamie nodded to Bree. She got out on the other side.

They both had their weapons ready as they moved forward, walking a few paces apart, ready to provide cover for each other. But all remained quiet as they passed by the house, checking it from the outside only, from a dozen or so yards away. The curtains didn't move, and there was no sign that anybody was watching them from inside, yet Jamie's instincts prickled.

They walked to the barn. Bree covered for him as he stepped inside into dusty darkness. They listened. No sound or movement anywhere in the dim interior. They turned on their flashlights to see better and panned the cavernous area in front of them. The stalls stood abandoned, farm tools and moldy hay taking up most of the space.

The old, wooden ladder to the hayloft looked promising, but rickety, to say the least, leaning more than a little. Bree tested it then shimmied up, keeping her gun out. She weighed less than he did. Still, he stood ready to catch her should the ladder break under her.

She disappeared over the edge of the hayloft. The wooden floor creaked under her as she walked around, checking every corner, sending dust sifting down between the cracks of the floorboards.

"Nothing up here," she called down before reappearing at the edge and climbing back down with care.

They left the barn and checked out the rest of the outbuildings. No sign of cars, although the grain silo was definitely big enough to hold a vehicle. Or more than one. It had no windows to look inside, and the door stood padlocked.

They moved on to the shed, according to plan. This they found unlocked. They went inside together.

The light coming through the open door and small window was enough; they didn't need their flashlights here as they looked around. Old, rusty equipment took up most of the space; things were piled randomly and perilously on top of each other. Jamie popped open the small window in the back and climbed through. Bree walked back out to distract whoever was watching them.

Keeping low, Jamie rushed over to the side of the house—no windows on this side, so nobody would see him—then moved around to the back. He stopped under the first window there and inched up. He saw a sparsely furnished bedroom, but there no sign of anybody and nothing was out of place.

Disappointment tightened his jaw. Maybe they were wrong about the old farmhouse. Maybe Swenson had gone someplace else.

He snuck over to the next window—open a crack—and popped up to eye level. This bedroom was just as deserted as the first one, but clothes lay scattered on the bed here.

Bingo.

He wedged his fingers into the opening and pushed the window up inch by slow inch, then climbed inside without making a sound, careful with his boots on the old, hardwood floor. He registered the clothes: faded jeans and a light shirt. Could definitely be Swenson's.

A duffel bag had been half kicked under the bed. He edged it open with his gun carefully and found more clothes, a box of ammo, some pill bottles and a stack of twenties held together by a rubber band, several thousand dollars' worth.

Things were looking pretty good.

He left the bag where he found it and moved to the closed door. Voices filtered in from the other side, at least two men talking.

Okay. They had Swenson, but the man wasn't alone.

Jamie pulled out his cell phone and sent a quick text to Mo, asking for backup. A month ago, he would have gone in, waiting for nobody. But he no longer needed to push the envelope every single time just to prove something to himself.

Now he had Bree, and that changed things, too. And Bree had Katie. So, no, he didn't always have to do everything the hard way. The smart way was better.

He put his phone away and turned the knob silently, hoping to hear what the men were talking about while he waited for reinforcements. Whatever intel he gained would come in handy later, and could be used against the men in interrogation.

"Nobody saw our faces," someone said. "And we had the license plate covered with mud. Ain't nobody gonna recognize us, no way. I'm telling you, man."

There was a long pause, and then a different voice said, "I can't take any chances. I'm sorry."

Then a gunshot, and Jamie had to sprint forward, because he knew the gunshot would bring Bree running.

He burst into the living room to find Steven Swenson holding a gun while a man lay bleeding on the floor, looking pretty much dead.

As Jamie burst in, Swenson swung the gun

toward him, his face startled, eyes wide. "Who the hell are you?"

"Put your weapon down! Customs and Border Protection," Jamie ordered.

Swenson's gaze darted back and forth, calculating. "Hey, man. I've been ambushed by a burglar. Clear case of self-defense. I'm an attorney. I'm not illegal."

"Put down your weapon."

Swenson hesitated, swallowing, measuring Jamie up, almost as if he was waiting for something.

What the hell was he waiting for? "Put down your weapon!"

Then the door banged open and another man came through, looking a lot like the one on the ground. They could have been brothers. The newcomer had Bree, one hand around her midsection, another holding a gun to her head.

As he took in the body on the floor, rage contorted his face. He yelled in Spanish, cursing Jamie and all his ancestors, assuming he'd been the one who'd fired the fatal shot.

"Calm down," Swenson advised, probably still thinking he could somehow come out of this clean if he only played his cards right. "Everybody calm down!" But he didn't sound too calm himself.

The guy with Bree didn't seem to be listening. His weapon hand was shaking as he swore at them all in Spanish.

The tension was escalating out of control, seconds from where it would hit conflict point.

And Jamie froze.

The bastard had Bree.

For a second, all he could think of was that family in the Afghan mountains. He couldn't save them. People on his team had called him a hero, but he hadn't been able to do anything heroic back with that family. He'd let them die. His fault.

And he blamed himself even more because nobody else wanted to blame him.

The only thing worse than being called a hero and put on a pedestal was being a failed hero.

And here he was again. The old darkness came back all at once and hit him hard. The thought of another failure paralyzed him. Bree meant more to him than he'd admitted, even to himself. And she was a split second from a bullet.

She looked at him with nothing but trust in her eyes. And at long last, in her eyes, he found himself. Not the overly tough guy he played to avoid pity, not the scarred mess he hid from others, but something truer and better.

His mind cleared.

"Hey." He lifted his hands into the air, but hung on to his weapon. "Nobody needs to die here."

The man holding Bree kept swearing, crying now, but Swenson looked interested. He shifted his weapon to his buddy. "You let her go."

As soon as Bree was free, he would shoot the guy, Jamie was pretty sure. Then there'd be no one to point a finger at him. Jimenez was gone, either lying low someplace or dead. Swenson would have nobody to testify against him.

"Everybody, put down your weapon," Jamie said in his best field-commander voice. "Let the deputy sheriff go." He shifted so he'd have a better angle on the guy who held Bree. She was not going to get hurt here, dammit.

"I have the right to defend myself in a home invasion," Swenson yelled.

His goon flashed a confused look at him. Swenson tightened his finger on the trigger.

He was going to go for it. And since he wasn't a professional, chances were pretty good he'd hit Bree by accident.

Jamie had to act first.

If he shot Swenson, the other guy would be startled and might pull the trigger on Bree. Which meant Jamie had to take him out now. Straight in the middle of the forehead was his only option, or he might twitch and squeeze the trigger before he died.

One, two, three. He held his breath, so even that wouldn't interfere with his aim, brought his hand and weapon down and shot at the bastard.

Unfortunately, Bree, having correctly read Swenson's intentions to make a move, did some self-defense maneuver at the same moment. She jerked forward with a sharp cry then dropped herself to the ground, which jostled the man as he grabbed for her, so Jamie's shot went into his shoulder.

The man shot at him as Bree rolled away behind the cover of an ancient recliner, even as Swenson shot at his own guy.

Jamie ducked behind the couch, hitting the lawyer in the arm on his way down. He couldn't go for a kill shot. They needed information from the bastard, dammit. He pulled his backup weapon from his boot and popped up long enough to throw it toward Bree, then flattened to the floor as a hail of bullets came at him.

Bree must have caught the gun because the next thing he heard was her yelling, "Freeze! Pebble Creek P.D. Drop your weapons!"

Jamie came up for another shot at Swenson just as the young gangbanger squeezed a shot off at Bree. Dammit, it was like the O.K. Corral in there. She shot back, springing up, but got hit, the bullet knocking her on her back.

Something snapped inside Jamie.

"Drop your weapons! Drop your weapons!" He rushed forward, yelling at Swenson. He was ready to put a hole in his head if he threatened Bree in any way.

The gangbanger was dead, he registered, lying in blood next to the other one. Bree had gotten him even as he'd gotten her.

Swenson shot at Jamie, missed, and then Jamie was vaulting on top of him, bringing him down, smacking him hard to make him go still.

"Bree?" he called back as he disarmed the man, flipped him, then handcuffed him.

"Bree?" He could turn back at last.

She was still on her back. His heart stopped.

But then she moved and sat up slowly. "That hurts."

And he could breathe again.

She was shaking her head and rubbing her chest through the Kevlar that had protected her.

"Man, I hate this part. It's going to leave a bruise, I know it."

He went over to her and helped her up. "Are you okay?"

"I'm fine. Let's finish this." She strode straight to Swenson.

"You have the right to remain silent." She

read him his rights while Jamie went to check on the bodies, checking pulses to make sure the men were as dead as they appeared.

Bree was back in cop mode, calm and matter-of-fact, pulling the lawyer to his feet, efficient as always while Swenson whined about the bullet that had gone through his arm, tossing out words like "police brutality" and "liability" and "legal protection."

She didn't let him rattle her one bit.

Man, she was hot in action.

Jamie wanted her. And it wasn't just the adrenaline rush.

He wanted her forever.

"All right," she said. "Let's take him back to the station."

He straightened. "Sorry. My team will want to talk to him first."

She narrowed her beautiful eyes at him, then relaxed her stance and gave a blinding smile that had his heart beating double. "I'm sure you agree—"

"Don't even try the sweet-talk thing. It's a matter of national security." Four SUVs tore down the driveway as he said that, all belonging to his team. He hoped they impressed his point on her.

"Fine." She didn't look happy, but she handed

Swenson over. "I can be reasonable. How about we share him?"

"Make you a deal. You can have him when we're done with him."

She was still smiling at him. "We make a good team."

Yes, they did. They were good together in every way. He needed to think about that instead of running away from it. But not now.

Mo, Ryder, Keith and Shep were jumping out of their cars and came running.

Chapter Fifteen

"I want the Coyote," Jamie told the man in the interrogation room.

The small space was hot, the air-conditioning cutting out from time to time. Swenson was sweating.

He had been protesting up a storm, demanding his rights and barely taking a breath. "I'm injured. I need more first aid than your idiot buddies handed out. This is the United States of America, not a third-world country. Who the hell are you, anyway? I'm going to be suing every single one of you for this unbelievable treatment. Count on it. You're going to answer for this."

He claimed he didn't know the two hit men at the farm. They were intruders, he'd said. He insisted that any shots fired by him had been fired in self-defense. If any bullets had come near Bree or Jamie from his gun, that was by accident. He was scared and he wasn't good with weapons.

"When are you going to let me go?" he demanded.

Jamie shook his head. "This is how it goes. I'm asking the questions here." He said the words slowly so Swenson would understand. "We'll stay right here, in this room, until you give me what I need. It's as simple as that."

"I have rights. I know the law. I want a lawyer." Swenson shot him another outraged look. He had quite a repertoire. He could have made a career on the stage. His acting ability had probably come in handy in the courtroom in the past, but was gaining him nothing here. He stomped his feet as he said, "I have the right to know what I'm being charged with."

Jamie drew his lungs full and let him have it. "Aiding and abetting terrorists."

That shut the idiot up.

He paled a shade. A moment passed before he fully recovered. "You're all crazy. I want my lawyer. I demand legal representation. That is my right as an American citizen."

"You'll find the procedures are different for a terror suspect. What do you know about the Coyote? When was the last time you saw him?"

Swenson shot to his feet. "We live under the rule of law in this country. I have rights." Apparently, he still didn't understand the kind of trouble he was in.

"Too bad you didn't remember those laws when you were breaking them."

"Do you understand who I am? I'm a prominent attorney in this county. I have friends who are judges and politicians."

Jamie stood, too, running out of patience. "Do you understand how little I care? Do you know how many good men I've seen ripped to pieces overseas by our foreign enemies? And then here you are, an American, and you're betraying your country? Want to know how I feel about that?"

He braced his hands on the table and leaned forward, his voice cold as he said, "I'm not a great fan of traitors. So here are your choices. Do you want to leave here alive or in a body bag?"

That got through to the man at last. His shoulders dipped, his words losing that tone of outraged superiority as he dropped back onto his chair. "I have no idea what you're talking about. I don't know anything about terrorists. I swear."

"Yet you work for a man who's setting up an operation to smuggle terrorists into the country. How far are you involved with the Coyote?"

More sweat beaded on Swenson's forehead.

"Look," Jamie told him. "This is about the last chance you have to be smart here. You don't want to further align yourself with him by protecting him."

The man swallowed hard and wiped his forehead with the back of his hand. The indignation on his face was replaced by worry lines and fear.

"All I know about is the counterfeit money. I swear. I didn't have a choice. When someone like that sends you a message that he wants your help, you help," he rushed to say, eager to speak now. "I want a plea bargain. I tell you about the money, you drop any charges that have to do with terrorism. There's no way you're going to pin that on me. No way."

He jumped up, but immediately sat back down again. "I want to cut a deal."

Jamie flashed him a dispassionate look. "I think you're under the mistaken impression that we're negotiating here. I want to know everything you know about the Coyote. Let's start with his real name."

"I don't know. I really don't."

"Where does he live?"

"I don't know."

"Here is a hint. You'll fare a lot better if you prove yourself useful to us. So let's try again. What do you know about the Coyote?"

The man stared at him, his entire body tight with tension, desperation in his eyes. "He tells me what he needs through messengers who come then disappear."

Jamie waited. "Solitary confinement," he said after a minute.

"What?"

"You give me that bastard and I'll arrange that you don't go into the general prison population." Meaning he might have a chance to survive the first week.

Swenson stared at him. Shook his head, but then almost immediately said, "Okay. Solitary confinement." He drew a deep breath. "I know where he'll be Monday morning. He needed to have something done. Medical. I hooked him up with a doctor friend who doesn't always keep patient records."

Somebody who was willing to take bullets out of criminals and gangbangers, most likely. What did the Coyote want with him? With the kind of money he had, he could have afforded the most expensive Swiss clinics. But the *why* wasn't as important as the fact that they finally had a straight link to the bastard.

Two days from now.

With enough information, they could set up an op to grab him. They would have enough time to make him talk, enough time to set up a trap for those terrorists.

For the first time in a long time, Jamie relaxed a little. The lack of progress over the past couple of weeks had gotten to them all. But now they had some actionable intelligence, finally. "Start talking."

This was it. They'd finally caught a break, and they were ready for it.

BREE LOOKED UP as Jamie walked through the door at dinnertime. He looked about as happy as she'd ever seen him. He wore blue jeans, a black T-shirt and his ever-present combat boots that she'd learned were fitted to his prosthetics to provide him with extra stability. He'd left his cowboy hat in his car. He was carrying a shoebox full of cookies.

"You bake?"

"Very funny. It was a gift."

"From a woman?" She hated the jealousy that bit right into her.

"I sent a young couple into the witness protection program today. She was grateful, that's all."

Just as long as they weren't going to see each other again. She took the box he offered and set it on the counter. They looked great—a bunch of different Mexican fiesta sweets.

"Any progress with Swenson?" she asked. "I want him when you're done with him."

"That won't be for a while yet. He's talking." He watched her for a second as if wanting to say more, but then he didn't.

Fine. She knew what kind of work he did. He'd never be able to share everything with her. She was okay with that. She understood it.

"We found the van that pushed your car into the reservoir," he said. "DNA evidence will link it to the two goons Swenson had at the farmhouse with him, I'm pretty sure. Ballistics already linked one of their guns to the bullet that killed Eleanor. Jason Tanner wasn't lying about not being the one who shot through your window."

She stared at him, various emotions mixing inside her. Jason's parents were in town and had made an appointment with her for tomorrow. At least she didn't have to tell them that their son was a killer. The family had suffered enough already, so she was happy for that.

Jason needed meds and to be in a facility where his movements were monitored. Mental illness wasn't a crime. He needed the kind of help he wouldn't be able to get in prison.

"So the men who shot Eleanor are dead. How do you feel about that?" Jamie asked, watching her.

"Good." While Jason had her sympathy, those two killers definitely didn't. They'd known what they were doing. They'd gone after her to stop her from investigating the counterfeit money business.

Jamie nodded, then looked around, up the stairs. "Where's Katie?"

"Over at Sharon's house for a sleepover. It's Sharon's birthday. Katie is not big on sleepovers, but she wanted to try. If I get a call in the middle of the night, so be it. I want her to have as many normal experiences as possible."

"She'll do fine. She's a sweet girl," he said. "How was your day?"

"All party and cakes. Mike had his retirement shindig."

"Liked his fishing pole?"

"You bet. I thought he might sneak out of the party to go and try it. It'll keep him out of Bertha's hair." Bertha was nearly as excited about the pole as Mike. She grinned.

Talking to Jamie like this felt nice: sharing their day, just being together without being in mortal danger.

He was standing in front of the living room window, which had finally been fixed, the late-day sunlight outlining his body—tall and wide shouldered. The man was pretty impressive, prosthetics or no prosthetics.

"A hero returning from the day's business." She said out loud the words she was thinking.

But instead of taking the compliment in the spirit in which it was offered, he frowned. "What are you talking about? I'm nobody's hero."

"You're mine. And I'm sure there are plenty of other people who feel the same."

"You don't know anything about my past."

"I know you've seen hard times. I know you risked your life for others."

"People died because of me."

"They shouldn't have plotted to attack our country."

He shook his head, a haunted expression coming over his face. "Innocent people."

"It wasn't your fault." She believed that with everything she was. He was good to the core, and honest and honorable.

"A whole family," he said. And then he told her a story that made her heart bleed and had her blinking back tears.

"The bastards went slow, made them scream. For days. And they would stop, they told me, if I gave them the location of my unit."

"They wouldn't have," she told him.

"I know. They meant to kill them from the beginning, to teach the rest of the village a lesson. And yet, I—"

"You couldn't have done anything to make a difference. If you'd given up information, more people would have died."

He rubbed a thumb over his eyebrow. "Sure, that sounds all reasonable and logical. Except in the middle of the night when I'm startled awake because I'm hearing their screams." He shoved his hands into his pockets. "I never told that to anyone before, not even the shrink at Walter Reed," he finished, and stood aloof, as if not sure how she would react.

She wanted to rush into his arms, but she wasn't sure if he would want it. Last time they talked about things between them, each had been adamant that there could be no relationship, nothing beyond the professional. Yet it was too late. They were friends, at the very least.

And more. If she said she felt nothing beyond friendship, she would be lying. "I wasn't sure you'd come."

He raised an eyebrow.

"Tanner is in jail. You have Swenson. His goons are dead. I no longer need a bodyguard."

"You never really needed one. I know you can handle pretty much everything yourself."

She narrowed her eyes. "Who are you, and what have you done with the real Jamie?"

He smiled. "I kept coming because I like being here with you."

Her heart rate picked up.

He looked at her, turning stone serious in a split second. "Do you want me to leave?"

Her heart sank. "Do you want to leave?" Then she laughed out loud. "I can't believe I just asked that. Could I sound more like a high school girl?"

The smile came back onto his handsome face. "I definitely don't want to leave."

"Good." She drew a deep breath. "Not that I have the faintest idea what we're doing here."

"We're having a relationship."

They were? "I didn't want a relationship."

"Me, neither. But I stand my ground even when I'm scared. Not that I'm scared. I'm just saying, in case you are."

"Really? You're going to play the 'who's chicken' card? Now who sounds like a high school kid? Where's the mucho-macho stuff?"

He came closer, caught her by the waist. He wiggled his eyebrows. "I can show you my manly ways. If you'd like."

"So you want me to ask for it? You think you're so hot you can make me beg? That's what you really want, isn't it?" she teased him, giddy with happiness that he was here and she was in his arms, that they had a whole night in front of them.

His gaze focused on her mouth. "I just want to stop you talking so I can kiss you," he said as his lips descended on hers.

He kissed so good. So unfair. How was she supposed to think and come back with some snappy response? Her knees were going weak; her brain was getting rapidly scrambled as he tasted the seam of her lips then teased his way inside, claiming her mouth fully.

She melted into his arms. There were times to be tough deputy chick, but this wasn't it. Her entire body tingled. She felt so incredibly good. Giddy, happy. She wanted this. She wanted him. She wanted more with every passing second.

When she was past all reason, he pulled back. Just enough to look into her face. He kept his strong arms around her waist.

His intense gaze held hers. "Why don't you want a relationship?"

"Oh, sure," she said weakly. "Ask questions when I can't think."

"I thought about it on the way over. I don't want this just to be a casual thing."

Nothing about Jamie Cassidy was casual.

"It's that…" she started to say, then stopped to figure out how to word it. "I'm pretty busy with work on the average day. And now we have sheriff's elections. Katie doesn't like change. If I ever got seriously involved with someone, I picture it as someone with a steady schedule and a stable job." She drew a deep breath. "Someone who might take care of Katie if something happens to me in the line of duty."

His arms tightened around her, his voice rough as he said, "Nothing's going to happen to you. That's an order. Do you understand?"

"You're not the boss of me."

His eyes narrowed.

She narrowed her own right back. "Your job is more dangerous than mine. As little as I know about it, I figured that much out. So if I can put up worrying about you all day, you can put up with worrying about me."

"Fine," he said, not looking the least bit pleased. "I care for Katie. I don't think she minds me. I would do anything to protect her. You know that."

She supposed she did, but hearing the words still made her feel better. "I've never seen her warm to someone as fast as she warmed to you. She has this sixth sense to know instinctually who's a good person. That's a big point in your favor. Among others."

He brightened at that. "There are others? What are they?"

She tried to pull away. He wouldn't let her.

Oh, for heaven's sake. "You do a fair job at kissing," she admitted reluctantly.

He pulled himself to full height. "Fair?" And then he dipped his head to hers and stole her breath away.

By the time he pulled back again, she would have admitted to being the tooth fairy, let alone that he was a good kisser. She probably looked fairly bamboozled, because he had a pretty proud look on his face.

"You're not bad yourself." He winked at her. "We'll figure the relationship thing out. I would do anything for you and Katie. You know that, right?"

This was the man who'd carried wounded teammates out of a war zone until he bled out to the point where he could no longer stand. Yeah, she believed him.

"Why?" she asked anyway.

"Because I'm falling for you." He held her gaze. "And I play for keeps. So let that be a warning."

Okay, he'd certainly laid his cards on the table. Warmth spread through her. Her heart seemed to swell in her chest.

"My life is never easy. Katie will always have to come first. I'm all she has. I'm responsible for her. You might not realize what you're taking on."

"I'll be around. I can promise that much. I'm permanently stationed on the border. But life is never a cakewalk. Mine has its own glitches."

Yes, it did. She so didn't care. She wanted him. So she reached up and, bold as you please, pulled his head back down to hers.

This kiss was softer, deeper, even more spine-tingling than the last, a confirmation of what they were feeling for each other.

He picked her up and her legs wrapped around his waist, his hardness pressing into her. He carried her toward the stairs, but she ran her hands up under his shirt as she hung on to him and they didn't make it.

He ended up pressing her against the wall in the hallway.

Heat suffused her as he rocked against her.

"Take off your shirt," he demanded.

She did.

He trailed kisses down her neck, to her collarbone, down into the valley of her breasts.

A moan escaped her throat.

"Yeah," he said, and brought up his hands to push her bra down, holding her against the wall with his pelvis.

Then his lips were on her nipple that was so hard, it ached. For him. And he did this thing with the tip of his tongue, a rapid back and forth movement that took her breath away. That was before he suddenly enveloped the nipple in the wet heat of his mouth and sucked gently. Pleasure exploded through her body.

She hung on to his shoulders for dear life.

Her entire body begged for him. She ground against him and he ground back, the need at her core intensifying to an unbearable level.

"We're not going to make it to the bedroom," he said in an apologetic, raspy whisper as he switched to the other nipple.

By that time, she could barely even remember that the house had another floor.

He teased her and suckled her until she was cross-eyed with need, tearing impatiently at his shirt, then at his belt buckle.

He slid her to the ground, but only until they had both stripped out of their clothing—in frenetic, jerky movements, working zippers with one hand, still reaching to touch each other with the other, their lips barely separating. Sweet mackerels, he was gorgeous.

He produced a small foil wrapper from somewhere and stumbled with it as he opened it without looking.

His body was carved from granite, every muscle perfect, and he had a lot of them. She wanted to touch him and never stop, her hands moving from his chest to his rock-solid abdomen and buttocks.

She couldn't help herself. Fine, she didn't *want* to help herself. She squeezed.

He groaned and lifted her again, up against the wall. She wrapped her legs around his waist, his hardness pushing deep inside her, stretching her, caressing her from the inside, filling her completely.

"Oh, wow," she said, barely able to catch her breath.

"You can say that again."

She simply moaned, because he began to move inside her and she was suddenly beyond speech.

The sex was amazing. He was amazing. Pleasure raked her body. She wanted to touch every inch of his skin and she wanted him to touch hers. She wanted his lips on hers and she wanted to never stop kissing.

Oh.

The man knew how to move.

Wave after wave of pleasure began where they were joined, then rippled through her body. Then the pleasure reached a crest and washed over her completely, her body contracting around him as she called out his name.

He stilled, held her, kissed her, caressed her. She'd barely come back down to earth when he started up again, a steady rhythm at first, then gathering speed.

She was utterly spent. "Jamie?" She couldn't take more of this.

Or could she?

Okay, she could, she realized as delicious tension coiled inside her all over again.

Then she remembered how long he'd been holding her up like this, how long he'd been supporting her weight. Did that feel uncomfortable for him? Was it hurting him?

"Do you need a—" Her breath caught and she couldn't finish.

But he somehow knew what she'd been about to say. "My legs never get tired," he said, and grinned. Then he pushed deeper into her, sending her body soaring all over again.

Later, when they were spent and both still breathing hard, she slipped her feet to the ground, and they leaned against each other, supporting each other, holding each other up.

"I want to say something."

"Okay." She pulled back so she could look into his eyes.

"You're the light of my life." He gathered her close against him. "I love you, Bree Tridle."

"I love you, too. But don't let it go to your head and get all protective. I'll still be deputy sheriff, even if I'm your girlfriend. So no putting on bossypants."

He laughed out loud before he kissed her. "No, ma'am."

* * * * *

Don't miss the exciting conclusion of
HQ: TEXAS,
by award-winning
author Dana Marton, when
SPY IN THE SADDLE
goes on sale next month.
Look for it wherever
Harlequin Intrigue books are sold!

LARGER-PRINT BOOKS!
GET 2 FREE LARGER-PRINT NOVELS PLUS
2 FREE GIFTS!

HARLEQUIN

INTRIGUE®

BREATHTAKING ROMANTIC SUSPENSE

YES! Please send me 2 FREE LARGER-PRINT Harlequin Intrigue® novels and my 2 FREE gifts (gifts are worth about $10). After receiving them, if I don't wish to receive any more books, I can return the shipping statement marked "cancel." If I don't cancel, I will receive 6 brand-new novels every month and be billed just $5.49 per book in the U.S. or $5.99 per book in Canada. That's a saving of at least 13% off the cover price! It's quite a bargain! Shipping and handling is just 50¢ per book in the U.S. and 75¢ per book in Canada.* I understand that accepting the 2 free books and gifts places me under no obligation to buy anything. I can always return a shipment and cancel at any time. Even if I never buy another book, the two free books and gifts are mine to keep forever.

199/399 HDN F42Y

Name	(PLEASE PRINT)
Address	Apt. #
City	State/Prov.	Zip/Postal Code

Signature (if under 18, a parent or guardian must sign)

Mail to the **Harlequin® Reader Service:**
IN U.S.A.: P.O. Box 1867, Buffalo, NY 14240-1867
IN CANADA: P.O. Box 609, Fort Erie, Ontario L2A 5X3

**Are you a subscriber to Harlequin Intrigue books
and want to receive the larger-print edition?
Call 1-800-873-8635 today or visit www.ReaderService.com.**

* Terms and prices subject to change without notice. Prices do not include applicable taxes. Sales tax applicable in N.Y. Canadian residents will be charged applicable taxes. Offer not valid in Quebec. This offer is limited to one order per household. Not valid for current subscribers to Harlequin Intrigue Larger-Print books. All orders subject to credit approval. Credit or debit balances in a customer's account(s) may be offset by any other outstanding balance owed by or to the customer. Please allow 4 to 6 weeks for delivery. Offer available while quantities last.

Your Privacy—The Harlequin® Reader Service is committed to protecting your privacy. Our Privacy Policy is available online at www.ReaderService.com or upon request from the Harlequin Reader Service.

We make a portion of our mailing list available to reputable third parties that offer products we believe may interest you. If you prefer that we not exchange your name with third parties, or if you wish to clarify or modify your communication preferences, please visit us at www.ReaderService.com/consumerchoice or write to us at Harlequin Reader Service Preference Service, P.O. Box 9062, Buffalo, NY 14269. Include your complete name and address.

HILP13R